A NEW MESSIAH

TONY NICHOLSON

GREAT ORTHERN

A New Messiah by Tony Nicholson

First published in Great Britain in 2022 by Great Northern Books

A CIP catalogue record for this title is available from the British
Library

ISBN: 978-1-914227-26-4

Design by David Burrill

Great Northern Books
PO Box 1380, Bradford,
West Yorkshire, BD5 5FB

www.greatnorthernbooks.co.uk

AUTHOR'S NOTE

A New Messiah is not a cautionary tale. It's unlikely to ever happen, although perhaps not impossible. It's a story which asks the time-honoured question "What if?" This particular "what if" has been buzzing round in my head for several years. I didn't have time to write it down however, because I was too busy making a living. Strangely though, just now, it seems particularly timely and 'of the moment', because it is fundamentally about the dangers of charismatic 'celebrity' political leaders gaining power. I don't think I need to name names, but there have been worrying examples on the global stage in recent years, from both sides of 'the pond'. On this side we had an amusingly bonkers public schoolboy buffoon who rose to fame bluffing, blustering and vacantly scratching his tousled head on the topical comedy panel game *Have I Got News for You*. Despite his widely-known, less than harmonious relationship with the truth, he then gained further mass fame, popularity and notoriety as 'a lovable rogue'. In all truth I think the last thing we need running the world are lovable rogues, thank you very much.

This story is set in an alternative version of the present day, or very near future. There is probably a lot you will recognise. Sadly so, in some cases. Some contemporary and very specific references will inevitably date quite quickly, but it seemed important to make it feel current and recognisable as every-day, as though this could be happening right now.

They always say write about what you know. I don't know too much about messiahs, I suppose, but I have spent most of my life around television and radio studios, working as both a TV producer and a scriptwriter. I worked mainly on entertainment programmes, and, over the years, I produced more TV magic shows than you could wave a wand at. In fact I earned my one and only, highly-prized, BAFTA Award for producing a TV magic show. So a lot of this story is about magic and magicians, and quite a bit of it is set in and around the world of television and the mass media.

While you are reading this you might like to play *Spot the Popular Culture References*. I have deliberately (and fondly) peppered the book with references from popular culture. I'll give you three random examples so that you know the kind of thing you are looking for. I refer to the central character, Serghei, in his street hustler days, viewing police arrest as "an occupational hazard". That is an affectionate homage to the words spoken by the judge, sentencing Fletcher to jail, in the opening sequence of every episode of the quintessential Ronnie Barker sitcom *Porridge*. In a later chapter Serghei's manager tells him, "The world was waiting just for you". That is a line from a sublime Beatles song, *Sexy Sadie*, which John Lennon somewhat bitterly wrote about his eventual disillusionment with The Beatles' personal Indian guru, Maharishi Mahesh Yogi. There is a fictional central London bar mentioned a few times, called Wonderland. That is simply named in honour of one of my favourite books of all-time, the splendidly inventive *Alice's Adventures in Wonderland* by Lewis Carroll. See how many more you can spot…

Please don't feel obliged to play along, but, if you do find a phrase or a notion which feels strangely familiar, you are probably right. It is.

Some of you may think that Serghei himself, my central anti-hero, is based on a real figure from recent popular culture. He's not. There are elements of several real people I have borrowed from, but an awful lot of him is made up, especially his many, many faults. However, it is true to say that the overnight fame and astonishing veneration of one particular celebrity magician, and the almost universal unquestioning belief in his 'God-given powers', did first make me ponder the question "what if…?"

Dedications

This book is dedicated to the fond memory of the
late and splendid Patrick ('Pat') Page – the most
knowledgeable magician I ever met, and a kind
and charming, but delightfully brusque Scotsman,
with a wicked sense of humour. I was proud to
work alongside him and call him a mate.

It is also dedicated to my wife Jackie,
and my sons Chris & Matt.

A NEW MESSIAH

CHAPTER ONE

Almost everybody in the United Kingdom was watching. Many in disbelief and horror, but most, it has to be said, with great excitement and fervour. There were huge video screens in parks and fields up and down the land where vast numbers of people had gathered to share the occasion. Every pub, bar and cinema had a live feed of the event. Ninety thousand people had queued, many of them camping overnight, to be there, actually in the stadium, where the devilishly-handsome, charismatic figure in dazzling white was spotlit at his lectern on the platform, garlanded with flowers. The baying throng were at fever-pitch, hanging on his every word. A collective mob mentality had set in, which made the heady zealous atmosphere positively intoxicating. Those that couldn't leave the house, or had young families, were at home, glued to their television screens, or were watching on their phones. The infectious sense of revolutionary change in the air was palpable.

"I have been given a purpose. God put me on this Earth that we might rise up and fight. It is time for change. Look around you at the evil of those who control us – our world leaders, our lawmakers, our law enforcers, our bankers, the heads of our corporations, even our religious leaders. Dishonest, morally bankrupt, corrupted by their immense power and selfishly steeped in sin... hypocrisy... greed... lust... hate... and lies!!!"

The powerful rhetoric, delivered with an unmistakable, but endearingly soft Eastern European accent, was heralded by a roar from the gathered crowd.

"The Christian Bible says, 'Naked I came from my mother's womb, and naked shall I return there. The Lord giveth, and the Lord taketh away'. Well you have given these pathetic greed-fuelled vipers the power that has become their venom, so you can take that power away! God sent them to this Earth naked and with nothing. Let us dispatch them to the torment of Hell naked and with nothing!"

Another roar of approval, and a shrewdly inclusive shift of gear:

"Muslim, Hindu, Jew, Catholic, Protestant – we are all united in this. Whatever your faith you have no need to fear the angels of death!

Redemption and forgiveness are guaranteed for true warriors of righteousness. The gates of any faith's Heaven will be flung wide open for those who kill or die in the fight for what is right. If our brothers won't join the fight for virtue then we must fight our brothers. Go back to your homes, unite as one with your neighbours and prepare to take up arms and take to the streets."

The crowd were with him all the way. They cheered ever louder as he asked whether they had the courage to fight. It seemed they had.

"We will rebuild a better Britain, but first we must tear down the walls and destroy everything that has gone before. I will lead you into battle if you will follow. Will you follow?"

The response was frenzied, but unequivocally yes.

There was chanting of "Serghei! Serghei! Serghei!" as the seething mob practically reached the point of hysteria. Scuffles were breaking out. A uniformed police officer crumpled to his knees, blood pouring from a gash in his forehead. Visibly armed, black-uniformed officials escorted the figure in white from the platform, still walking with a pronounced limp.

The reaction from the rest of the world was predominantly that of helpless bewilderment, much like on the inauguration day of President Donald J. Trump. Of course there were those from other nations who not only approved, but were positively envious.

How could it have come to this so quickly? How could it have come to this at all, in a habitually benign, introverted and largely unflappable nation?

Barely four years ago this new messiah was being incarcerated in a Romanian prison, and not for the first time. Nothing serious, but short jail sentences were an occupational hazard for somebody who hustled the streets to make a reprehensible living. Scuffles and affrays were almost inevitable. Once again a burly punter had taken exception to losing a street corner game of 'Find The Lady', and had punched Serghei squarely in the face, attracting the attention of passing police, who were all-too-familiar with Serghei's tricks, and had little sympathy. Usually Serghei's 'better half' Aurelia bailed him out of prison. You could be forgiven for calling it a bribe. However, she'd had enough and, this time, refused to pay up. Serghei was powerless and had to serve seven miserable days in a hot, dingy, cockroach-infested cell with an unwashed and evil-smelling pickpocket. As Serghei pointed out to the weaselly little fellow – it's a wonder his victims didn't smell him coming.

On his release he reclaimed his sunglasses, watch, ring, keys, bracelet, mobile phone, his ever-present pack of playing cards, and his wallet, which was now empty. The guards viewed it as a perk of the job, as they knew the money actually belonged to some other poor suckers who hadn't had the good sense to punch Serghei in the face. As he swore at the guards for this unprovable theft they just laughed and suggested that, as a magician, he could just conjure up some more money to replace it. One helpfully suggested that he should perhaps have followed his father into a profession. The trouble was he had done just that.

Blinking in the bright spring afternoon daylight, as he re-emerged back into the world and freedom, he looked all around, and then at the dusty road ahead. No sign of Aurelia, and it was a long way into town for somebody with no money for a taxi. There was just enough charge left on his mobile to phone home, but Aurelia refused to come and pick him up. She told him in no uncertain terms that she couldn't take this lifestyle any more. Serghei managed to counter with a reminder that his late mother had always said she was a prize bitch, before his phone finally died on him. He swore profusely again as he started to walk. After a few minutes a lone cattle truck rumbled up behind him, but his outstretched thumb was ignored and the truck left Serghei eating its dust. His obscene gesture and screamed profanities made no difference. It didn't come back.

Almost three hours later, dirty, sweaty and exhausted, and sporting a week's unkempt beard growth, he finally arrived at their front door. It was already dusk, but he could see that there was a new, unfamiliar-looking lock surround, which appeared incongruous against the faded, peeling paint of their ageing wooden door. Even so he felt obliged to try his key, which of course didn't fit. His banging on the door, however loud he hammered, received no response, so, once again, his only available course of action was yelling and swearing, this time through the letterbox. At long last he did get a response, though not a particularly polite one, from the woman across the road.

In desperation he went around the back of the tightly-packed, crumbling row of houses to the rough spare ground where he parked his car. At least he could sleep in there until Aurelia emerged the next morning. The last straw was seeing his rusty old Skoda propped on bricks by a wheel thief. Serghei let out a self-pitying roar of anger and despair.

Four days later a huge lorry rumbled off the ferry at Dover and the French driver drove to a motorway service station to refuel. Puzzled by the muffled banging coming from the back of the ostensibly empty cargo unit he flung open the rear doors and nearly leapt out of his skin when a dirty, dishevelled figure with a holdall pushed him aside and ran off across the forecourt, disappearing into the massive car park. The shocked truck driver just stood there shouting and cursing after him in the kind of French you certainly don't learn at school. Unwanted, uninvited and somewhat unlawfully, Serghei Iliescu had sprinted his first inauspicious steps of this fresh start in his new motherland.

Sleeping rough at first, Serghei had gravitated towards the capital city, where he found he could make a much better reprehensible living than he ever could back in Romania. He quickly learned that the working people of London were dismissive, disinterested and cynical, but the plentiful passing tourist trade in Leicester Square was more gullible, more genteel, more affluent, and much less likely to punch him in the face than his countrymen back home. 'Find The Lady' or 'The Three-Card Monte', as it was sometimes known in England, proved to be an easy and highly profitable tax-free scam. The American tourists were the best. They would believe that the closer they watched the more chance they had of finding the Queen, so they would linger longer, and lose more. Like the best bookies he would allow them the odd small win, which encouraged them to continue gambling and lose even more times. Time and time again Serghei's dazzling dexterity as a first-rate magician proved the hand really could be quicker than the eye. Not only that but, if all else failed, his astonishing sleight of hand was not averse to facilitating a good measure of cheating. More often than not, when the naïve punter made his or her selection, there wasn't a lady there to find. The increasingly dog-eared and well-thumbed three playing cards on top of the wooden box, covered with a grubby square of green baize, were eventually replaced by three half walnut shells and a dried pea. It was the same scam, dressed up differently. As the money rolled in the dried pea and the walnut shells were in turn replaced by three shiny brass cups and a red ball from a local magic shop. Still the same scam, with even less chance of winning, as any magician worth his salt will tell you. The original stakes of fifty-pence pieces had become one- and two-pound coins, and, occasionally, the odd five-pound note. On a good day, weather permitting, Serghei could rake in fifty pounds an hour. About the same as a good dentist.

The police usually turned a blind eye. There was far too much paperwork involved to bother with somebody who was, to all intents and purposes, harmlessly entertaining the visitors in The West End's most famous square. In any case the visitors weren't complaining, and most of them could afford to lose.

It wasn't long before somebody with Serghei's undoubted skill, cunning, self-belief and arrogance had made enough money to rent a small bedsit, and buy an old banger to get around in. His bad-boy charm, mysterious accent and dark smouldering Romany looks also ensured that he very soon had a seemingly endless string of girls on his arm. As a faux feminist he was more than happy to let these female admirers splash their cash on him and do the entertaining at their places, rather than his. His complete lack of any sort of conscience ensured he had no guilt about that, or about moving swiftly on to the next conquest. He'd always had an insatiable libido, which was one of the many reasons Aurelia had finally decided enough was enough.

It had been a highly successful and enjoyable summer. Serghei Iliescu's life could have meandered quite happily and contentedly along like that for a very long time, but a chance encounter that sunny autumn was the start of a bizarre chain of events, which would snowball beyond belief, and not how anybody could have ever predicted.

As usual on a Saturday morning Serghei was in Leicester Square, now at a proper baize-covered card table, reverting for old times' sake to 'The Three-Card Monte'. His elegant, manicured hands were flicking the crisp, brand-new playing cards around with his usual astonishing dexterity, when an equally elegant hand reached in and turned over the Queen, much to the gathered crowd's delight and Serghei's obvious chagrin.

"You are a magician, yes?" snarled an unamused Serghei, under his breath.

"I am, as a matter of fact, yes."

"Then sod the fuck off!"

Rather than doing as he was told the other magician came closer, secretly pressing a folded ten-pound note into Serghei's hand, whispering covertly:

"Let me win this back, then just watch the stakes go up…"

Grudgingly Serghei allowed the young man to win back his tenner, but then, sure enough, others in the crowd became eager to bet as much as ten pounds, and, equally sure enough, they lost. Serghei had a very lucrative run, watched encouragingly by this new pop-up helper.

Packing away his cards, folding up his table, and pocketing his considerable winnings, Serghei was determined not to thank this other magician for his uninvited help, or even acknowledge it. He certainly had no intention of sharing his ill-gotten gains. However, he did somewhat unenthusiastically agree to having one drink in a nearby bar with the rather staid-looking, young, bespectacled man, who had introduced himself as Clive Entwhistle. But only then when Clive made it clear that he was paying.

It didn't need a body language expert to detect that it wasn't exactly a comfortable social occasion. Drinks in hand, the conversation flowed like bitumen. Serghei was still determined not to thank Clive for his profitable intervention.

"I work alone, my friend."

Clive looked slightly hurt. "So do I. I wasn't auditioning for a job. But I did help you make some extra money."

"I do just fine."

"You can't work the streets for ever. Our winters are too bloody cold, for a start!"

"What are you, my mother?"

There was another awkward lull in the conversation, then Clive hit on a talking-point which always bonds and unites magicians – magic. He asked Serghei if he could do a 'Zarrow Shuffle'. Seeing the Romanian's puzzled expression Clive produced a deck of cards from his jacket pocket and, with several ostentatious but impressive flourishes, he appeared to shuffle the deck thoroughly. He then turned the cards over to show that they were all neatly arranged – all the diamonds, clubs, hearts, spades grouped together, in perfect numerical order.

Serghei nodded, trying not to look too impressed. "Ah, yes,

I don't know name 'Zarrow', but I know the move."

He then took the cards from Clive and, in an unashamed bit of one-upmanship, he did some even more flashy shuffles and turned the cards over to show they were still in exactly the same order. All except the four aces which somehow had made their way to the top of the deck. Pushing the aces back into the middle of the stack of cards he shuffled again and, lo and behold, the aces had this time, miraculously, found their way to the bottom of the deck.

"Bloody hell!" said Clive. "You're wasted on the streets doing 'The Three-Card Monte'! Do you do anything else other than cards?"

As all magicians know full well, these showy displays attract attention. Other customers in the bar were now gathering around them, especially young women. Serghei's rugged allure made a good deal of the attention gravitate his way. He took a few coins from his pocket and started rolling them around his knuckles with astonishing skill. His banter came easily, making up for what it lacked in political correctness with endless cheeky charm. As he put on a small show for the gathered girls his testosterone-charged charisma drew them in like moths to a flame. Serghei's brooding bad-boy looks, cool unsmiling demeanour, topped off by his enigmatic Eastern European accent, clearly created a potent aphrodisiac. One attractive, flame-haired girl in particular seemed to have swallowed the bait. Serghei rewarded her enrapt and flirtatious attention with a gift from his inside pocket. A sparkly gold-plated watch. Her own watch in fact, which he'd somehow spirited off her wrist, without her knowledge, and surreptitiously pocketed whilst performing an earlier coin trick for her. She couldn't believe her eyes and appeared to melt visibly.

Suddenly and surprisingly Serghei turned his back on the group of girls, who were still squealing and cooing over his latest miracle with the watch, and blatantly asked Clive to buy him another drink. Here was a man who knew what he wanted and how to get it, and didn't much care whose feathers he ruffled in the process.

"Don't turn your back on the girls – I think you're in there," Clive said, somewhat naively.

"Of course I am, my friend. Don't sweat it. She will get even keener if I make her wait."

Clive, not exactly a man of the world or a 'player', looked bemused, but bought the drink, as instructed. "I think I could get you some magic work at parties," he said, over the noise of the busy bar.

"Oh no, my friend. I do not pull rabbit out of hat for screaming kids covered in snot and jelly."

"No, neither do I!" laughed Clive. "I've got a big wedding to do next Saturday. I need someone to do it with me. It'll be a piece of piss. A few coin and card tricks for each table, then move on. We'll be in and out in an hour or so. Two hundred quid."

"Each?"

"Two hundred for you – a little more for me, as it is my gig."

Just then the attractive, flame-haired girl tapped Serghei on the shoulder, exactly as he had predicted and planned, and asked to see another trick. He didn't need asking twice. Slipping an arm around the girl's waist Serghei downed his drink in one, ungraciously turned his back on Clive, and walked off with her. Clive gave chase and pressed a business card into the Romanian street hustler's hand, telling him to phone, then watched him leave, half irritated by his new mesmeric acquaintance, and half in awe of him.

"Have you got a suit?" Clive suddenly called after Serghei, as an afterthought.

CHAPTER TWO

The wedding went well. The well-heeled guests were suitably entertained by the two magicians who circulated all around the sumptuously-appointed marquee during that awkward wedding day gap after the meal and the speeches, but before it was time to change for the evening disco. The tipsy guests were especially beguiled by the dark handsome one with the mysterious accent. They found themselves able to turn a blind eye to his somewhat tacky, cheap silver suit and fake-leather cowboy boots, distracted by his eye-popping conjuring skills and endearing audacity. As Clive had said they were in and out in just over an hour with a small wad of cash each, in hand.

This new magical double act was short-lived, however. Like any pact with the devil there was a catch. On the Monday morning Clive was walking to the supermarket and getting ever more irate. In a fit of pique he phoned Serghei, who was nursing a hangover in a greasy-spoon café, tucking into a ketchup-laden sausage sandwich and a mug of sweet tea.

"So I've just been called by the wedding planner. The very pissed-off wedding planner, as it goes. Apparently two guests lost expensive watches on Saturday. She can't prove anything of course, but she knows as well as I do where they mysteriously vanished to! You wanker! How could you let me down like that?!"

Serghei listened impassively, then answered through a mouthful of half-chewed sandwich, "What are you trying to say, my friend?"

"Don't call me your friend. I am not your friend! I give you a break and you disappoint me by betraying my trust!"

Serghei's eyes narrowed and he snarled into his phone,

"Let's face it, you wanted me to disappoint you. You'd have been disappointed if I hadn't disappointed you. You wanted to play God and give the immigrant street urchin, bloody gypsy boy, his big break, but deep down you secretly hoped he would let you down. Well, fuck you, I never asked for your charity."

"No – fuck you – that agent says she'll never use me again. I have lost a whole load of work because of you!"

The conversation then descended into a juvenile exchange of 'fuck yous' which increased in volume, until Clive got a reproachful look of disgust from a woman pushing a toddler in a buggy in the opposite direction.

So ended a brief and not so beautiful friendship.

Clive harboured a grudge and kept running through it all in his brain, over and over again, feeling hurt, betrayed and angry. Serghei shrugged, finished his cholesterol-packed breakfast, and never gave Clive another thought.

However, Serghei was the one who had benefitted from the experience, and not just from what the local 'Cash Converters' gave him for the watches. It had opened his eyes to a more lucrative, less weather dependent and surprisingly honest way of using his well-honed magical skills to make money. Soon he was working the thriving London circuit of corporate dinners, weddings, bar mitzvahs, and private functions. The very circuit, in fact, that had provided Clive with a steady living for the past ten years.

By the end of the year word-of-mouth had turned Serghei into a regular fixture on the close-up magic circuit. New Year's Eve was always a good night for magicians to pick up a reasonably well-paid gig, and most of them would sacrifice their own merry-making to entertain inebriated revellers. Both Serghei and Clive were out working, but at opposite ends of the partying capital.

Serghei, still wearing the shiny silver suit, but thankfully not the cheap cowboy boots, had been booked for a mid-range private party in a large three-star hotel function room, packed with middle-aged, middle-class people who felt they were too posh to stand along the Thames watching the fireworks, but not posh enough to afford the really prestigious dinner-dances which were going on in Mayfair. As usual he had metaphorically charmed the pants off the guests with his ever-expanding close-up magic repertoire, which now included impressive mind-reading feats and using his 'God-given mystical powers' to bend spoons from the tables. The punters were loving it. The catering manager was slightly less keen.

It was still well before midnight and Serghei had taken a break from working the tables to attempt to more literally charm the pants off one of the younger single women at the party. They were standing at the bar, with Serghei working his magic in more ways than one. She was slightly inebriated and was clutching a playing card to her chest, willing Serghei to read her mind.

"You are strong independent woman, so I think the card you choose was a high card – a strong card…"

She was lapping it up, grinning and nodding encouragement.

"You are very passionate, yes, so it is a red card. You are romantic though, I can tell, so it must be a heart."

"Yes!" she beamed.

"A heart, I knew it. Now close your eyes and think very hard about your card. Picture it in your mind. Concentrate!"

As the acquiescent young woman closed her eyes, Serghei took the opportunity of sliding out a letter, which was protruding slightly from her open handbag. He took a furtive glimpse and quickly pushed the letter back in, having seen all he needed to see. The envelope was clearly emblazoned with a logo for 'The Dogs Trust', and he had been able to spy her name and address through the translucent window.

"You are the Queen of Hearts, yes?" he announced, dramatically.

She squealed with delight, revealing the card she had been clutching to her bosom was indeed the queen of hearts. "Yes! How did you guess that?"

Serghei took her hands and parroted some typical magician mumbo-jumbo about not needing to guess because she exuded such a strong aura that he could read what she was thinking. In truth of course he knew she was going to choose the queen of hearts before she did, and then made sure, using sleight of hand, that she did choose it.

Serghei pulled her closer and whispered furtively, "I was part of Russian military research programme into harnessing psychic powers."

"Oh wow! You worked in Moscow? The Kremlin?" she cooed.

"I am not permitted to talk about. I have already said too much."

The young woman giggled and made a jokey comment about him meeting a sticky end with a poison-tipped umbrella, but Serghei glanced over her shoulder, then pressed his finger to her lips, shaking his head earnestly.

In close now he gazed into her eyes as though he was searching for a glimpse into her soul. "You are very caring person, I think. Look at me. You like dogs, no?"

"How did you know that?"

"I told you. You have very strong aura. You don't just love dogs though – you help them I think…"

"Yes, I do charity work helping rescue dogs," she said, wide-eyed in wonderment at this seemingly miraculous insight.

The magician's tried and tested seduction technique was about to reach the grand finale. Serghei gently pulled her ever closer.

"I knew you were caring person. Look into my eyes. You live in North London. Hampstead, I think. No. Highgate! And your name it begins with a 'J'. Jeanette perhaps – no, it is Jennifer, yes? Like Jennifer Anniston, and just as beautiful."

"Yes! Jenny really." She was blushing now.

Unfortunately for Serghei the spell was abruptly broken by the sudden close presence of a redoubtable, full-figured woman in her fifties, who looked reproachfully at Serghei and instructed her daughter to return to their table as her father was wondering where she'd got to. Had Serghei had any long-term plans for a serious relationship, the mother might have been a portent of things to come and forewarning that perhaps Jennifer might not age as gracefully as her namesake, Ms Anniston. However, he had no intentions whatsoever beyond that evening, so he cursed quietly to himself, downed his drink and went off to mystify another table full of men in ill-fitting dinner jackets and women giving their gaudy jewellery its annual airing.

Meanwhile Clive Entwhistle had finished his allotted Hogmanay stint at a pseudo-Scottish function a few miles away, and had managed to slip away, before the bagpipes, the sword and the flaming haggis, in time to bring in the New Year with his mother back in their simple West Ruislip flat.

His mum Molly, a plain, drably-dressed woman, who looked and behaved considerably older than her sixty-odd years, had spent all evening in her favourite armchair, by the television, half-watching a drearily depressing hour-long episode of *Emmerdale*, and a dismal so-called 'comedy' film from the 1970s, with Burt Reynolds in Bermuda shorts and an orange wig. With toasty feet, thanks to her new fluffy slippers, and both bars of the electric fire blazing away, she was dozing, the small tumbler of sweet sherry in her hand in danger of spilling its contents onto the threadbare rug.

The musical door chime woke her with a start, a little sherry splashing on to her second best floral frock. Molly whispered the mildest of curses, which was actually quite profane, coming from her. Anxiously, not expecting any callers at this late hour, she went to the door and put on the security chain, opening the door just a crack.

"Who is it? What do you want? I'm not on my own. My son's in," she said, trying to sound convincing.

"Yes you are, and no he isn't! I'm out here!" chuckled Clive.

"Oh it's you, you silly beggar!" she said, closing the door to unlatch the chain, and then inching it open. "What have you done with your key? You frightened the life out of me!"

"I'm First-Footing. You have to answer the door and invite me in. Happy New Year! … Hurry up – it's cold out here."

"It's only twenty past eleven!", his mum said, craning round to look at the kitchen clock.

"Your First Foot comes bearing a wee dram, courtesy of the Caledonian Society," Clive continued, undeterred, showing her a miniature dimpled whisky bottle. "I think I'm supposed to have a lump of coal and a piece of shortbread as well, but you'll have to make do with your favourite – a walnut whip from the garage on the corner."

His mother beamed, flashing her dentures, and told him what a good lad he was.

"It's flipping cold out here, Mum! You have to invite me in!"

"Well come in then, you silly devil – you're letting the heat out!"

Clive took off his coat and hung it up, revealing his smart performance suit. Molly was already back by the fire, rubbing her hands together. Cracking open the whisky miniature Clive explained that he had managed to get away from his gig early, saying that he hated working New Year's Eve because everybody was so drunk they could never remember which card they'd picked. Molly in return told him what she'd been watching on TV, trying unsuccessfully to explain the tenuous plot of the unfunny Burt Reynolds film. She suddenly realised the ending was a complete mystery, even to her, as she'd nodded off. It was one of those conversations where neither party is remotely interested in what the other is saying, but both still nod and show polite interest.

"Did you really come home just to see your old mum?" Molly asked.

"Course I did!" Clive answered sincerely, pouring her the tiniest nip of whisky.

"Oh you are a good boy!" she said, kissing him sloppily on the cheek as he leaned down towards her with her glass.

Serghei had just finished impressing another table at his function, with his big finish – bending a spoon with the 'power of his mind', much to the irritation of the catering manager, who was rapidly running out of spoons. As ever somebody at the table enquired about the extent and scale of his paranormal abilities, and, also as ever, he evaded giving an answer by putting his finger to his lips, saying, "The Kremlin won't let me talk about it. I have already said too much…"

The enthralled party-goers were left feeling special because the mystical entertainer had apparently shared some international indiscretion with them. In fact, he'd said absolutely nothing. It was an extremely clever ploy.

By ten to twelve the guests were getting too drunk to amaze, and were by now eagerly anticipating the midnight chimes of Big Ben, so Serghei had retired to the bar for another well-earned drink, disappointed that he hadn't managed to make a conquest to help him celebrate the first new year of his new life.

It suddenly became apparent to Serghei that he was being joined by a well-groomed, not unattractive man in his forties, wearing an expensive pinstriped suit. The debonaire effect was somewhat spoilt by the ostentatious addition of garish 'bling' – a chunky gold bracelet, several oversized rings on both hands, and a huge Rolex-style watch.

This chance encounter was to become a major stepping-stone towards Serghei Iliescu's unexpected deification. Another one of those seemingly inauspicious moments which somehow change everything, irreversibly.

The stranger spoke in a brash but husky, cockney-wideboy accent, carefully cultivated over many years to impress, amuse, survive and intimidate in equal measure. His opening gambit was simple and to the point: "You're not bad, my son!"

Being patronised twice in just five words irritated Serghei immensely, so he ignored this damnation with faint praise. There was an awkward pause before Serghei looked the man up and down and said, "You don't look like dinner-dance type. Why you here?"

"You're the fortune-teller. You tell me…"

"Oh, like I never hear that one before!" snarled Serghei, rapidly losing interest in any further conversation.

The stranger shrewdly changed his approach. "So you were part of some Russian military research programme?"

Serghei, as usual, wasn't particularly interested in anybody other than himself or an attractive girl, so he didn't look at the man, mumbling his perennial get-out that he wasn't permitted to talk about it.

"Well you've talked about it to just about everybody in the whole place!" came the perceptive deadpan response.

Serghei didn't rise to the bait, taking another sip from his drink, but the self-consciously flashy man persevered. "It's just I know Putin. Vlad. I provide the entertainment when he or Abramovich bring a yacht into the Med. Girls mainly." Failing to even raise an eyebrow he changed tack yet again. "Gaga would love you, you know…"

"Who?"

"Gaga. Lady Gaga to most people. She loves all this other-worldly crap. You'd freak her right out, you would, my son."

They say it takes a thief to catch a thief. Well the same sort of thing applies to people who have a flexible relationship with the truth. Serghei was not buying this blarney. "Look, my friend – you have a saying in your country, right? Don't kid a kidder…"

"What are you saying exactly?" the smooth operator said, looking all hurt and wounded, feigning righteous indignation.

"I am saying what we both know. You don't know Vladimir Putin and you have never met 'Gaga'. Save your breath for some gullible sucker – somebody who might give a shit."

Sneaking admiration was now beginning to creep in, but the stranger wasn't about to admit it. He wanted to prove that he could also smell hogwash from a mile away. "Bit rude! I let you not tell me all about your research for the Russkies. I'm assuming that's a load of old pony as well. What do you say if somebody spots you're Romanian, not Russian? You are

Romanian, right?"

Serghei shrugged indifferently. "The Kremlin throws its net wide, my friend. I just say I work for highest bidder. That much is true."

It was rapidly becoming apparent that these men, whilst totally different in temperament, were actually kindred spirits, cut from the same cloth.

The stranger knew from bitter experience that life was too short to waste too much time on lost causes, so he cut to the chase. "What you need is a good manager, my son. Maz Masters. I have my own club."

Maz Masters reached out to shake Serghei's hand. In a smooth move, perfected during a lifetime of avoiding the appearance of being the underdog in slippery business dealings with much more intimidating adversaries, he quickly spotted that Serghei wasn't going to reciprocate with a handshake, so he deftly turned the outstretching of his own hand into a flamboyant motion to produce a gold business card from his jacket pocket, with a flourish. Pressing the card into Serghei's hand, he said something far more prophetic than either of the two men could have ever imagined. "Together we could rule the fucking world!"

The historic moment passed almost unnoticed because, just then, the plump middle-aged DJ, with the dated blonde highlights, came on the microphone, instructing everybody to make their way to the dance floor and form a circle as midnight was rapidly approaching. The two men were caught up in the ensuing surge of people, with Jennifer making a detour to slip a napkin into Serghei's pocket with her phone number written on it in lipstick. Right at that moment the red-blooded magician was far more interested in the inscribed napkin than Maz Masters' business card, even though the latter was on course to change his life.

"Call me, yeh?" Jennifer smiled, dutifully heading back to her parents, just as the DJ started playing his trusty old mini-disc recording of Big Ben's chimes, thirty seconds too early. Of course this slightly premature celebration didn't matter one jot to the cheering, inebriated throng who were about to caterwaul the same few half-remembered lines of 'Auld Lang Syne' twenty times over, because nobody actually knows the words.

Clive and Molly were sipping whisky, which neither of them really liked, whilst watching the spectacular firework display on TV, broadcast live from the River Thames, having just wished each other a Happy New Year as midnight chimed. Clive suddenly noticed that his mother had big tears rolling down her rosy cheeks, so he put his hand on her wrist, making sympathetic noises, and telling her not to cry.

"I can't help it. New Year brings it all back. I still miss him so much."

"I know you do." Clive patted her hand. "But he wouldn't want you being all upset. Here – come on…" he said, pouring her another drop of whisky.

"There's not a day goes by that I don't think about him. Do you?" Molly enquired, more in hope than anything.

"From time to time, yes, of course, but it's not like he was my dad."

"Don't talk to me about that waste of space!" snapped Molly.

Clive really didn't want to get into this, but she couldn't stop him talking to his own father, whatever he'd done when the two of them were still married. In fact he'd just texted his dad to wish him a Happy New Year.

"Don was more like a father to you than he ever was. Or ever will be!"

Clive wanted to say something, but wisely bit his tongue. It caused a bit of a hiatus though in their conversation. Fortunately the fireworks on TV provided a distraction.

"Well I know what my New Year resolution is going to be," Molly suddenly announced.

"I don't get the point. Nobody ever keeps them."

"I will. I'm going to make a real effort this year to contact Don."

Clive rolled his eyes. "Oh God, no mum! Not all that old claptrap again! I've told you they're all just a bunch of thieving con artists!"

Clive, with his knowledge of magic, was well aware of the tricks and scams so-called clairvoyants and spirit mediums used to fool grieving and vulnerable people into parting with their hard-earned cash.

"You're wasting your money, and what for?" he asked in an exasperated tone.

"Peace of mind, that's what for! Closure. And you don't know everything, you know. Chrissie from bingo, she went to see that Liverpudlian one a few years ago, Derek Acorah. She said he was unbelievable."

Unbelievable just about summed it up for Clive. And if he was so good how come the late Mr Acorah hadn't been back by now with a reassuring message from 'the other side'?

The whole subject had been a bone of contention between Clive and his mum ever since the death of Don, his step-father. Mother and son fell silent. Happy New Year.

CHAPTER THREE

With New Year come and gone, the festive season now over, Serghei had found Maz Masters' cheesy, gold-coloured business card in his pocket. He had to grudgingly admit to himself that he had felt some affinity towards the flashy individual. There was certainly no harm listening to what he had to say.

The two men were sitting at a VIP table on the front row of Maz's club, with Serghei in his ever-present shiny silver suit. Clutching bottles of over-priced lager, with bass-heavy music pulsing monotonously, they were intently watching a near-naked young woman snaking her perfectly contoured, fake-tanned body around a gleaming silver pole.

"I'd give you a residency here, but you could pull a bleedin' dancing elephant out of a hat, yank a bunch of flowers out of its trunk, and then make it disappear again and none of these randy fuck-wits would notice," Maz said, competing manfully with the music. "But here's the deal. You promise me you'll stop scamming the streets with the 'Three-Card Monte', and in return I promise you I will never send you out for less than four hundred quid."

Unblinking, Serghei just continued to watch the erotic gyrations of the dancer, as though he wasn't really listening. After a good few moments he suddenly reached over himself to shake Maz's hand. Maz started to reciprocate, but then hesitated as he laid down two final conditions to the creation of this unholy alliance.

"Oh, and you have to promise me you'll stop nicking stuff from the punters… and you'll get another bleedin' suit! I'll have that one melted down and made into a new pole for the girls. You couldn't even give it away to a dosser. Nobody'd buy a *Big Issue* off of some dude dressed like Robocop!"

Serghei looked puzzled, but continued to shake Maz's hand. He recoiled slightly though when Maz pointed out that he'd be taking twenty-five per cent commission.

"Don't get cheap on me now, Serghei! That was the cut Brian Epstein got from The Beatles. The day he signed them he promised he'd make them bigger than Elvis. Well I'll make you bigger than…" he hesitated as he racked his brain for the name of an international mega-star magician.

"David Blaine?" prompted Serghei, hopefully.

"The Great Soprendo!"

"Who?"

"Exactly…"

To avert any further discussion on the matter Maz quickly beckoned to Tiffany, an extremely attractive blonde girl, who was hovering near the fire exit, wearing precious little more than sparkly tassels and high-heeled shoes. He instructed her to give his friend a free dance, on the house. As Tiffany slowly and seductively pulled Serghei to his feet by his bootlace tie, and led him towards a private booth, his mind magically drained of all thoughts of contracts, percentages, promises or degrees of potential future fame.

* * *

A few weeks later the dynamic duo were sitting in the back of a black cab, with Serghei now immaculately dressed in a designer suit and tie, just like Maz. As always he was absent-mindedly, but impressively riffling through the deck of cards that were rarely out of his hands. They were discussing how the night had gone, Serghei secretly thrilled at earning six hundred pounds for just over an hour's work, even if it did mean giving his new manager a hundred and fifty of it.

"Good to break into that corporate market," said Maz. "That's where the big bucks are. Six hundred tonight but we can build on that."

Serghei said he was more than happy with six hundred, but Maz assured him that six grand was better and, more importantly, perfectly possible.

"But I think you should junk the 'Pick a card, any card' crap. There are thousands of magicians out there who can make a signed ace o' spades appear out of the managing director's wife's left ear'ole. Where you have 'em wetting their knickers is with all that getting into their heads stuff."

The habitually inflexible Serghei bristled, "I am the performer. I never let people tell me what to do."

"No, and you've never earned six hundred notes before!"

"I am good with cards…"

"You and all the other ten-a-penny table-hoppers. But we can make you a unique 'brand'. Special. When you screw with their heads it puts you in a different league, my son."

Maz then tapped on the dividing window in front of him and asked the cabbie to drop him off on the left at the next corner but one.

"We should forget anything that makes you look like a magician. And I think we should drop your surname. Nobody can remember it. And when they can remember it they can't pronounce it. In any case 'Iliescu' sounds like a trademark on a porcelain urinal."

His new client appeared unimpressed, sarcastically asking if he should perhaps change his name to 'Serghei Smith'. Maz ploughed on, regardless, suggesting that, from now on, he should go out working simply as 'Serghei', "Because it sounds dead mysterious."

"Serghei is common name in Romania," he grumbled, almost sulkily.

"So 'Trevor' is probably more mysterious in Romania!" Maz opined, easily matching Serghei's earlier sarcasm. "Tell you what – we'll put you out as Serghei over here, and Trevor when you play the Bucharest Palladium!"

You could almost hear the cogs turning in the magician's head, as he tried to compute the undeniable logic behind these radical life-changing proposals. He frowned and questioned the whole idea of being known by just a single name.

As ever Maz had a ready answer. "It worked for Jesus…"

Just then the cab stopped and Maz leapt out, pushing a twenty-pound note through the driver's open window, telling the cabbie to take the gentleman in the back wherever he wants to go. The driver looked disparagingly at the twenty-pound note and snorted at the suggestion.

"Don't worry. He's loaded!" countered Maz. "Just look at his suit…"

* * *

It didn't happen overnight. There was a period of uneasy negotiation. Both men were used to getting their own way, and neither of them were very good at doing as they were told. Maz Masters was far from an academic, having left school unqualified at just sixteen, but twenty-plus years of crawling his way up through the somewhat seedy underbelly of Soho had given him a street-smart intelligence, which can't be taught at school. Through necessity he had also learned to turn persuasion into a fine art. Serghei didn't stand a chance. Pretty soon the card and coin tricks were disappearing from his performances, making way for the astonishing feats which appeared to happen through 'the God-given powers of his mind' – mind-reading, predictions, telepathy, spoon-bending. Of course, in reality, these 'miracles' were just as much sleight of hand and magical illusion as every card trick he had ever perfected.

And the single name 'Serghei' was beginning to be spoken about with wonderment by the chosen few who had seen him perform. Just as Maz had wanted and predicted.

Something which did almost happen overnight, however, was Serghei's infatuation with Tiffany, the blonde lap dancer from Maz's club. He fell head-over-heels for her stunning physical charms right from their first intimate introduction. She liked him too, and was quickly seduced by his smouldering looks, bad-boy allure and his magical skills. House rules said the girls weren't supposed to date the punters from the club, but Maz made an exception for his protégé, who wasn't actually a paying client anyway. Serghei was allowed the rare privilege of knowing her real name – 'Tiffany' just being her working lap dancer stage name. She was twenty-six-year-old Simona Novak, from a small suburb of Prague in the Czech Republic. She'd had a tough upbringing, which she refused to talk about, and had escaped to England at the age of just seventeen, pretending to be slightly older. Right from the start her body, natural long blonde hair and perfectly symmetrical Slavic features had proved to be her meal ticket. Glamour modelling had soon led to being a popular regular at various sleazy gentlemen's clubs around London. She had quickly found that Maz's club was her favourite, because, despite his lairy wideboy image, he always treated the girls fairly and with respect. He also paid them well. His philosophy in business had always been not to selfishly cream off a larger share of the pie for himself, but to make the pie bigger so everybody got a decent slice. It was a methodology that had always served him well and had earned him undying loyalty from his often world-weary employees.

Simona's English was by now near-perfect, but she still had an appealing Eastern European accent, which made this particular exotic dancer seem even more exotic. Within weeks Serghei had somehow managed to persuade Simona to let him move in with her. She had a much roomier and more sumptuously appointed modern apartment than him, almost overlooking the Thames. Her popularity in her chosen field had made her a top earner.

Whatever Serghei's many shortcomings, he was always a hard worker, and he seemed to never stop rehearsing, devising and developing new routines to amaze his audiences. His latest 'paranormal' departure was telekinesis – the apparent ability to move solid objects using nothing but the power of the mind. The

Russians and Americans had both done research into various claims of telekinetic powers, or 'PK' – psychokinesis. One American psychic demonstrated that he could make a round pencil roll away from him on a flat table by just looking at it, and could also turn pages of a book by simply staring closely at them. Only after putting him under laboratory conditions did they discover that it wasn't his mind that was controlling the objects, but his mouth. He was silently blowing a small controlled jet of air between his front teeth to make these things happen. Similar PK claims had been debunked in Russia, but the public were always far more interested in the claims than the exposure of any fraud, so they continued to believe that there must be some truth in these sensationally captivating reports of 'paranormal powers'.

It was nearly noon – crack of dawn to a lap dancer and a magician – and Serghei was hunched over the large glass-topped coffee table with items of cutlery dancing and spinning around underneath his hands. He was concentrating so hard on mastering this new trick that he didn't even notice Simona approach, wearing nothing but one of his shirts. Ever the sceptic she came closer and stooped to check the gap between Serghei's open palms and the randomly moving forks and spoons.

"You have strings!" she said, annoyed that she couldn't see how he was achieving this unbelievable effect. She was even more annoyed when she grabbed his wrists and forcibly turned his hands over, only to find a complete absence of 'strings'. Serghei was too good a magician to be exposed so easily.

"How do you do that?" Simona demanded.

"I am in league with the devil," he joshed, almost prophetically.

Simona started grumbling about him spending more time thinking about his magic tricks than he did thinking about her. He tried to explain that Maz wanted him to learn how to do more supernatural feats and tricks of the mind, which needed lots of concentration and rehearsal. Simona, however, didn't seem particularly impressed by that excuse.

"You know what Maz's real name is?" Simona suddenly grinned at her own non-sequitur. "I saw it on an envelope in his office one day…"

"No. He always calls himself Maz."

"Stanley!"

Their giggles relieved the slight tension in the air.

"No wonder he calls himself Maz!" Serghei said, smiling.

"So Stanley wants you to become a psychic?"

"Not psychic, no. But he says mind-reading tricks and this paranormal stuff cuts me apart from the rest. Makes me different."

Simona pouted provocatively, a clever trick she herself had perfected over the years, and pointed out that his mind-reading skills must be sadly lacking if he wanted to play with dancing cutlery while she was thinking such horny thoughts. It worked. She suddenly had Serghei's undivided attention.

"Let's go back to bed and have some fun. It will be late when I get back from work tonight," she purred.

What was it Shakespeare said about the course of true love never running smoothly? Simona's stark reminder of her work set Serghei off once again on his new crusade to rescue her from such depravity. In truth his so-called moral outrage was simply a case of macho possessiveness, combined with an unhealthy dose of masculine hypocrisy. He'd been perfectly happy to ogle her and the other girls gyrating their near-naked bodies at Maz's club, but, now Simona was his girlfriend, he didn't want other men doing the same. Of course Simona, a worldly-wise strong woman, could read him like a book. She certainly didn't need 'rescuing', and she resented the implication that she should be ashamed of how she made her not-inconsiderable living, from which he was now benefitting.

She put Serghei straight in no uncertain terms, reminding him that he'd only been around for five minutes, and she'd managed perfectly well without him for many years, making her own decisions.

"I just don't like to see you exploited," he whinged unconvincingly. "I don't want you to go tonight."

"Don't patronise me, Serghei! I am not exploited."

"All those losers trying to grope you…"

"And there it is! You just want to think you own me. God gave you your talent, and he gave me this body. Gave it to me, not you. So I use it to pay for all this. My choice! Nobody tells me what I can and can't do."

Serghei couldn't think of a clever enough response, and he wasn't man enough to apologise, so he looked away and started setting up the table to rehearse his trick again.

"And don't sulk like little boy. Go to the fridge and open something with bubbles before I change my mind," Simona said huskily, shrugging off the shirt and letting it drop to the floor. Somehow she was managing to wear nothing and the trousers all at the same time.

This was to become the pattern of life for the next few months. Maz gently, but successfully, inching Serghei away from life as a traditional magician, towards a specialism in 'feats of the mind', thus totally transforming his perception as a performer, by stealth. And Serghei trying to inch Simona away from life as a lap dancer, but failing miserably. As both the manipulated and failed manipulator Serghei was still able to convince himself that he was in complete control of his own destiny. This arrogant self-belief, combined with a total lack of awareness of being stage-managed himself, was a lethal cocktail which would soon form a recurring theme in his imminent and meteoric rise to fame and power.

Around the same time Molly, Clive's mother, was actively searching for a spirit medium to conduct a séance so that she could contact her dear departed second husband, Don Hill. This fact, seemingly unrelated and inconsequential, was actually significant as part of the overall butterfly effect which helped to trigger the momentous chain of events which was about to change everything for everybody.

CHAPTER FOUR

Word of the mysterious Serghei and his 'God-given powers of the mind' spread like wildfire, the flames fanned by Maz's relentless efforts to blitz the media with publicity stunts and embellished stories. On a day when there was little real news Serghei quickly became a reliable column filler for the tabloid press.

The mythology surrounding him was helped by word-of-mouth. People who had seen him perform would exaggerate or misremember exactly what they'd seen, their overblown stories making him sound even more impressive than he really was.

It wasn't long before television producers started to take notice, but Maz shrewdly waited for the right offer to come along.

Serghei was understandably edgy as he sat by the lightbulb-studded mirror in the plush ITV dressing-room, waiting to make his first major appearance on British television. He was nervous, not that he was about to admit it to anyone. His understandable jitters made him irritable and sullen. It was a big deal for a newcomer to be appearing alongside Hollywood royalty, comedy giants and music legends on *The Jonathan Ross Show*. The audience were in their seats, and the warm-up comedian was settling them in and making them feel receptive and comfortable, before introducing the legendary chat show host.

Into Serghei's dressing-room sauntered Maz, adorned with all his showiest bling for this momentous evening. His ebullient mood was struck a blow when Serghei turned and snapped at him.

"What in hell do you think you are doing?"

"Whoa! Hang on there champ!" Maz said, making a show of bringing up his arms in mock defence. "What am I supposed to have done?"

Serghei petulantly described how a young excitable female assistant producer had just come to his dressing-room saying that Maz had told her that he was not to be introduced as a magician, because his magic was magic of the mind; a God-given psychic gift he'd been born with. Serghei made it painfully clear that he still felt uncomfortable with this deceit, especially on such a high profile appearance as this.

"Listen, my son. I got you on television, didn't I? It's one of the biggest shows around. 'A-list' Hollywood stars queue up to be on here. They turned Tom Cruise away last week because he didn't meet the height restrictions."

"Everything is joke with you," groused Serghei.

"Not anything to do with money or business. Look, if they're stupid enough to believe you're for real – bleedin' well let 'em, I say!"

Serghei was not mollified by his reasoning. "I'm not some emissary of God, you arsehole! I'm a fucking conjuror!"

Maz looked anxiously over his shoulder and signalled with his hands to quieten Serghei down. "You didn't tell her that, did you?"

Serghei shook his head. "She didn't let me get a word in. But I want to succeed on my talent as magician, not be seen as some kind of freak in circus sideshow. You had no right telling her those things."

Maz looked up to heaven in disbelief. "What about all that Russian military research programme crap you come out with?"

"That is just to get laid. This is important to me, as a magician. I don't want people thinking I'm claiming to be some kind of prophet."

"Nothing wrong with profit," muttered Maz, almost to himself. "Look, just avoid the words magic, magician or trick. That's all I'm asking. Indulge me. Roll with it for today. We'll have this discussion later."

Serghei wasn't giving up, rolling up the sleeve of his tailored shirt to reveal a small black gizmo strapped to his forearm. "This is electromagnet, not hand of God. All psychics are crooks and frauds anyway."

"So what's your problem? One more won't hurt."

Serghei rolled his sleeve back down and went into a sulky silence for a few moments, lost for words. Then he told Maz that the assistant producer had asked him to do a psychic reading on Jonathan. "I am going to bend a spoon and stop his watch. That's not quite the same thing!"

Maz adopted a more soothing tone, needing to pour oil on the obviously troubled water.

"Look, just do what you do and we'll talk about this tomorrow. Oh, and I've just been chatting to Jonathan's mum in the Green Room. Lovely woman. Dead chatty. When he was a little boy he wanted to be a bus driver, and he had a gerbil called Gerry."

"I'm a fucking close-up magician!" stormed Serghei.

"Just saying!" Maz grinned, ducking out of the door to allow Serghei to calm down and get his head together. He'd planted the seeds, he could do no more.

The Jonathan Ross Show studio audience loved Serghei. There were audible gasps when the metal spoon in his hands started to bend before their eyes. Next he dramatically donned protective goggles and a heavy-duty glove to hold a lightbulb out in front of him, staring at it intently. Some of the audience actually squealed with shock when the lightbulb noisily exploded, before they exploded themselves into tumultuous applause. It was going perfectly. Maz was watching a monitor in the wings, grinning from ear to ear with pride. You could almost see the dollar signs in his eyes, like a 1950s cartoon character.

Serghei had now borrowed Jonathan's wristwatch and was holding it over his thigh, concentrating hard and murmuring, "Stop. Stop. Stop…"

The audience almost held their breath. Letting out a sudden theatrical gasp, as though it had taken every ounce of his inner strength, Serghei thrust the watch back at Jonathan.

"Oh wow!" exclaimed the host. "It's stopped! It really has stopped! That is amazing, ladies and gentlemen!"

The audience went wild.

Jonathan looked at his watch again, then out at the camera, as though taking the viewers at home into his confidence, and grinned cheekily, "I know it says it's a Sekonda, but, if it won't start again, for insurance purposes, it's a Rolex, right?"

The audience enjoyed his smart ad lib. Things couldn't have been going better.

Jonathan sat back in his chair, in obvious admiration, and then asked what was inadvertently a turning-point question for everything which was to follow.

"When did you first discover that you had these abilities, these powers, or whatever you call them, Serghei? When did you start doing this stuff?"

It was a defining moment. Maz stopped grinning and leaned towards the monitor, anxious to hear the response. Serghei didn't answer right away, unnerving Maz. He was clearly considering coming clean that everything he had just done were nothing but magic tricks.

Serghei looked Jonathan in the eye for a moment, then said, "At school…"

Maz let out a huge sigh of relief and discreetly punched the air with delight.

Jonathan took the opportunity of cracking another spontaneous gag. "Just what you want in your class! Somebody who makes the clock stop! Playtime never comes. Couldn't you have made it go faster?"

The audience's warm response gave him a few moments to put his wristwatch back on, but Serghei suddenly stopped him and grabbed his wrist, staring directly into his eyes. Once again Maz held his breath.

Out of nowhere he started, "When you were in school you

wanted to be a driver, I think. Not racing car driver like most boys though. Something big, like a truck or a train. No, a bus..."

You could see the genuine surprise and awe in Jonathan's eyes. "Get out of here! How did you know that?"

"And you had a school friend called Gerry, I think..."

Jonathan shook his head, clearly disappointed. "No, there was a Gary, but he wasn't really a mate..."

"Well then Gerry was an imaginary friend."

Jonathan got another laugh by saying, with mock indignation, "I was a very popular child, I'll have you know!"

Serghei didn't smile, but kept staring unnervingly into his eyes. "Gerry was definitely with you back then..." Serghei frowned, then suddenly looked as though a revelation had hit him between the eyes. "No, wait! Gerry wasn't a boy. He was pet. But not big pet like cat or dog. Small. Like mouse or hamster maybe?"

Jonathan shook his head in admiration and disbelief. "A gerbil, actually. How on earth did you know that?! You know, ladies and gentlemen, I was pretty sceptical when my producer told me about Serghei, but, I tell you what, he's the real deal, this guy! Let's hear it for – Serghei!"

The audience applauded loud and long, with Maz looking absolutely elated in the wings, like all his Christmases had just come at once.

Two days later Clive Entwhistle and Molly, his mother, were watching *The Jonathan Ross Show* recording being transmitted on ITV. They were clearly getting very different experiences from the same programme, both watching open-mouthed, but for completely different reasons.

After Serghei's rapturous exit Molly turned to Clive and said, "I don't care what you say, Mr Know-It-All, I think he was marvellous!"

Clive was scowling uncharitably. "He's just a magician. I know him."

"So you keep saying."

Molly reminded her son that Serghei had indeed admitted to Jonathan Ross that he'd done a few magic gigs in the past, as a way of paying the bills. It was a clever way of covering his tracks as there were plenty of people around London who had seen him working at parties and functions as a close-up magician. The best lie is always a half-truth.

"He's the one nicked those watches from that wedding," Clive snarled with undisguised bitterness in his voice.

"So you say!"

"Oh what? You think I stole them? Thanks a lot, Mum!"

Molly scolded her son and told him not to be silly. "You can be very childish, Clive Entwhistle, when you don't get all your own way."

There was an awkward silence during Molly's favourite TV advert with the singing dog, then Clive muttered, "I'm just saying that he doesn't have mystical powers", adding with a sneer, "A so-called gift from above".

Molly took his cynicism for envy, which wasn't completely off the mark. She reassured her son that his time would come, suggesting, for at least the thirtieth time, that he should give that *Britain's Got Talent* a try. "You could win that."

"I'm not jealous of him. I just don't like him conning the public. He's nothing more than a good sleight of hand merchant, and an even better street hustler."

Molly Hill frowned disapprovingly, quoting one of her bingo night pearls of wisdom, "There are more things in heaven and earth than are dreamt of in the minds of men you know. You've become very cynical since your magic took off, Clive Entwhistle. And it's not an attractive quality."

Clive snorted and shook his head, feeling quite aggrieved that his own mother should side with the enemy.

* * *

The morning after the triumphant broadcast Maz and Serghei

were standing at the bar of Maz's club. During daylight hours, with the house lights on, the place looked even seedier, and actually quite grubby. A large middle-aged woman with a cigarette hanging from her bottom lip was noisily hoovering the sticky carpet tiles, and a toothless man of indeterminate age appeared to be deriving slightly too much satisfaction from polishing the silver pole on the stage. The empty cavernous place, now devoid of punters and pulsating music, echoed eerily, and there was a lingering smell of sweat, beer, toilets and testosterone, mingled with cheap disinfectant.

A pile of newspapers stood on the bar, between an extremely smug Maz Masters and Serghei, who, despite his best efforts to remain indifferent, couldn't help looking rather pleased with himself. Maz patted the stack of tabloid papers, every one of which carried a headline or a major story about the TV mystic making his astonishing debut on *The Jonathan Ross Show* the previous night.

"Now I'm not going to say I told you so. Oh, hang on, I tell a lie. I am going to say I told you so. I fucking told you so! Have you seen the papers?"

Unable to hide a self-satisfied grin, Serghei said, "They liked me, yes?"

"Liked you?! They fucking loved you, my son!"

The palpable excitement triggered Maz's default mode – verbal diarrhoea.

"I've already had the breakfast telly people on, but it's a bit bloody early to get up, and there's a real danger that Piers fuckin' Morgan might have got his job back. Although I've always fancied giving that Lorraine Kelly one. Maybe we should reconsider. *This Morning* want you to see if you can read Phillip Schofield's mind. That shouldn't take too fucking long. But I think we should hold out. See if one of the TV companies offer you your own special. Don't want to over-expose you. Burn you out. You are suddenly a red-hot property, my son!"

Just then Simona strolled up, dressed casually, but sexily, in skin-tight jeans and a sweater. Over her shoulder was slung her work bag, which seemed ludicrously spacious for a couple of tassels and a pair of high heels.

She greeted the two men, "Hey Maz, hey babe…"

"Hi Tiff!" grinned Maz, genuinely pleased to see one of his favourite employees.

Serghei bristled slightly, "Simona. Her name is Simona."

"She's Tiffany when she's at work, aren't you darlin'?"

Serghei looked unhappy at this reminder, but caught Simona's warning look and decided, wisely, to bite his tongue.

Maz pretended not to notice the obvious friction and made small-talk about Simona's presence at such an early hour.

"Doing the lunchtime session today, hun?"

"Saturday afternoons always pretty good" she said, shrewdly capitalising on her extensive experience. "Drunks are best tippers."

Serghei looked even more infuriated at the implications of why these drunken lechers were such good tippers, but again knew better than to ask or comment.

Simona went on to explain that it would also mean she would be home for 'Mr Sulky-Boots' that evening. She asked Maz if Serghei had been trying to play it cool about the reaction to his big television debut.

"Well he did manage a fleeting smile at one point."

"He was up at seven to get newspapers," Simona said, spilling the beans. "Then he came back in bedroom dancing up and down like he'd won lottery."

"I think he probably has sweetheart."

At that moment Maz's phone sounded loudly. His ringtone was a tinny sounding synthesised version of 'Brown Sugar' by The Rolling Stones. He barely looked at his phone before cutting the caller off.

"What you doing?" Serghei said, with a horrified expression. "It could be something important."

"I bleedin' well hope so!" Maz countered. "But it doesn't pay to be too readily available. The more important it is, the more likely they are to call back, and then I can tell 'em I was talking to the BBC."

"What if it was BBC?"

"Then I'll tell 'em I was talking to Channel Four for fuck's sake! Deary-me! You need me more than I realised. I'm not charging nearly enough."

Maz turned to Simona and asked her to run along, saying he needed a private word with Serghei. She nodded agreeably and turned, with Maz launching her off with a crisp smack to the seat of her skinny jeans.

In any other workplace, that controversial act would have been considered totally inappropriate and arrestable, but was still the time-honoured norm in a lap dancing club. It has to be said though that the girls were still very much in control. If the wrong person tried such a thing they'd wake up on a saline drip.

"Hey man! What the fuck's that?" Serghei demanded to know, not so cool with this locally accepted practice.

"Oops, sorry my son. Getting a bit keen are we?"

Serghei explained that he hated Simona working at the club and wanted her to quit.

"Listen. A word to the wise. I wouldn't try telling her what she can and can't do. She'll be up that pole tomorrow night wearing nothing but your bollocks as earrings."

Relationship advice was not, however, why Maz wanted a private word with Serghei. This was something much more important. He looked around furtively, as though he thought somebody might be listening in, then pulled Serghei closer, speaking in a low voice.

"Apart from you and me, who else knows how you did what you did on that telly show?"

Serghei stroked his chin and pondered for a moment, pointing out that other rival magicians would inevitably have their theories.

"Theories, right, but who else knows for certain that it wasn't for real?

I mean really for certain. Did you confide in anybody?"

Serghei shook his head, then said, "Simona has seen me

rehearsing. I talk to her about it."

"What the fuck did you tell her for?" gasped Maz, in exasperation.

Serghei queried why he shouldn't discuss things with his own girlfriend.

"Look," said Maz, suddenly serious, "I really think we're on to something here. Something massive. But it could all tumble like the proverbial house of cards if somebody blows the whistle. So you didn't say anything to anybody at the TV studio?"

Serghei reminded him that a magician never reveals his secrets.

"Good. So from now on you tell nobody. Understand? Nobody. The sceptics can all have their theories and take their shots at you, but no one can prove anything if only you and I know the truth. And that's the last time ever you refer to yourself as a magician, right Serghei?"

"So what in hell am I supposed to call myself?"

"I dunno. A paranormalist or something. You can call yourself the new Messiah for all I care. Anything except a bleedin' magician! It means whatever gobsmacking stunt or miracle we aim to pull off we've got to take care of everything just between the two of us. No stooges or collaborators. So nobody can ever come out the woodwork and blow us out the water."

"So I have to be like in spy movie? I'd tell you, but then I'd have to kill you."

Maz raised an eyebrow. "So Romanians do have a sense of humour? I had been wondering." He thought for a moment, then checked, "That was humour, right?"

Before Serghei could answer Maz's phone rang again. This time he took the call, with a flourish.

"Maz Master's voice," he said, then listened. "Yes, that is correct. I'm his business manager. Just hold for a nanosecond love." He held the phone away from him and then shouted off at his non-existent personal assistant that he was on an important call. "If it's *The One Show* again tell 'em to fuck off. We've got bigger fish to fry!"

He then went back to the real call, apologising for the 'interruption', and explaining that the phone lines were white hot today, as he was sure she could imagine.

CHAPTER FIVE

Clive was sitting watching *Countdown* on television, when the door opened and in bustled his mother, all dressed up, with a silly grin on her face. She waited for a moment and then could not contain herself any longer.

"Aren't you going to ask me how I got on?" she beamed.

"You know what I think about it all," Clive wearily sighed.

"Well it just goes to show that you don't know everything, because it went really well, as it happens. The spirit medium was marvellous. He were a bit strange, but ooh, he were ever so good."

Molly went on to regale her cynical son with a blow-by-blow account of the séance she had attended that afternoon. Her memory of it was heavily influenced by rose-tinted spectacles, which enabled her to blot out the overwhelming smell of cat urine and cabbage which engulfed her as she walked into the dingy flat. She had also chosen to forget the unseemly eagerness of the medium wearing tartan carpet slippers to get his payment before she'd even taken off her coat. There had been others there when she arrived, mainly women of a similar age, already keenly assembled around the candle-lit table, which was covered with a drab brown damask cloth.

The flat had been decorated nicely in the 1970s, but hadn't had so much as a lick of paint since, so all the magnolia and cream was now a sort of nicotine-sepia. It was incredibly chintzy, with three-dimensional ceramic cherubs and seraphs drooping from hooks on the wall, their gold paint flaking and darkened with age. There were also glazed pot dogs lined along the mantelpiece over the tiled fire surround; and yellowing lace antimacassars draped over the back of an overly fussy floral three-piece suite.

Cecil Goodchild, the medium, was small and stooped, with false teeth which looked as though he'd inherited them from one of his deceased spirit visitors, with a much bigger mouth. The loose denture plates clicked every time he spoke, and seemed alarmingly in danger of slithering out at any moment. His cut-price, canvas-based toupee had obviously been bought before the remaining side bits of his real hair turned wispy grey. Perhaps that's why he greeted clients by nothing more illuminating than candlelight. When he spoke it was with an old-fashioned camp timbre, not quite hiding a decidedly acid twist.

Molly had sat spellbound as he made them all join hands, before closing his eyes and chanting twice, "Our beloved spirit friends, we bring you gifts from life into death. Commune with us, and move among us."

The spirits obliged with surprising speed. Cecil was quickly possessed by five of them who, coincidentally, just happened to be the souls of the late lamented husbands, partners and loved ones of the five people sitting around the table. The spirits thoughtfully waited in turn to possess Cecil, who was working in a strictly clockwork rotation.

Each visitation from the other side followed a similar pattern. A couple of points of recognition to astonish the living person, and convince them that the spirit in question was indeed their loved one. A reassurance that said soul was doing just fine in the spirit world, and not suffering; followed by a comforting message of hope and positivity about their eventual reunion.

It has to be said that all five paying clients left feeling uplifted and filled with joy. So where's the harm in that?

There are three schools of thought on the morality of Cecil's controversial trade. Either he has a genuine gift and is providing a wonderful service; or he is a harmless fraud who is innocuously offering spurious, but nonetheless positive pastoral care for the bereaved; or he is a confidence trickster who is cynically exploiting vulnerable people who are already suffering.

Clive was firmly of the third school of thought. Being a magician he knew the many methods by which such séances can easily be faked, and was very vocal on the subject. It is a common crusade amongst professional magicians. The great Houdini spent the last years of his life righteously debunking fake séances and exposing fraudulent psychics and mediums. On his own death-bed he promised his wife Bess that, if there really was a means to do so, he would come back and speak to her from the other side. He said he would quote a secret code word so that she would know it was him. She religiously held a carefully controlled séance every Halloween, the anniversary of Houdini's death, but he never did contact her. Of course you could argue that his spirit could easily have chatted away to Bess every year, but Houdini preferred to keep quiet because he didn't want to prove himself wrong.

Clive couldn't help himself from picking holes in his mother's story. Cecil had correctly quoted Don's unusual middle name, which very few people knew; he had identified where Don was born and went to school, his sister's name and even what he died of. All of these hard facts had totally convinced Molly that Don was indeed there, speaking through Cecil.

"When you booked the appointment for today did he ask what date Don died?" queried Clive.

Molly was defensive. "It was a woman answered the phone, not him. I suppose she might have asked that, but I didn't even mention Don's name, so how could he know all that stuff if it wasn't Don speaking? I just told her I wanted to contact my late husband."

"They file away all the obituaries from the local papers. All he needed was your name and the date."

His mum was starting to get emotional. "Don channelled a message through him. It were lovely. He says we haven't to worry about him, he's fine, although he misses me. But he says it's not my time yet. I have more destiny to fulfil here on Earth before I can be reunited with him on the other side."

"Funny that," muttered Clive, "I don't ever remember Don

talking like some dodgy vicar from an old black and white film."

Molly answered in a trembling voice, "I wish you could be more pleased for me!"

"And I wish you'd come to your senses and stop throwing money you can't afford at these thieving crooks!"

Molly burst into tears and fled the room. Clive suddenly felt remorseful and chased after her. "Mum! I'm sorry. I didn't mean to upset you. Look, what do you fancy for your tea? Do you want me to get us some fish and chips?"

* * *

There was a frisson of excitement in the plush hotel function room where the press had gathered. Cameras whirred, clicked and flashed as Maz Masters led Serghei in to take their place at the table on the podium.

Journalists secretly enjoy press calls like this. They are much less dull than Government briefings, and much less harrowing than police statements on terrorist attacks or missing children. And it didn't hurt that some of the showbusiness-based press conferences, like this one, offered a free glass of wine or two afterwards. Not only that but Serghei was filling column inches and selling lots of newspapers. This was a story they actually all wanted.

Maz stood and welcomed everybody, thanking them for coming, then introduced himself, making much of his successful few months as Serghei's personal manager, and carefully avoiding mention of his many years as the proprietor of a lap dancing club. He then waved towards his astonishing protégé and invited questions. Eager hands immediately shot up, with Maz selecting the most friendly faces.

"Serghei – can you explain how you are able to do the things you do?"

Serghei adopted the enigmatic expression which had worked so well for him throughout life. "I wish I could. All I can say is it's like big energy force within me. I didn't go looking for this,

I just discovered I had these powers. This gift."

Several voices were unsurprisingly prompted to ask whether he could do something for them now.

Maz intervened, as though it was his fault, so that Serghei didn't appear uncooperative, "It's very draining when he uses this inner energy force, so we agreed no demonstrations this morning. Sorry guys."

Another journalist followed up this train of thought by asking Serghei how it made him feel when he used his powers.

"It makes my whole body tingle. Not unpleasant feeling, kind of warm. But it leaves me emotionally exhausted, as Maz say."

A young female journalist asked Serghei to list the things he can do.

"I can move solid objects, just with power of my mind. I think you call that telekinesis, or PK. Some solid objects I can bend or even break, just by concentrating on them. I also have some telepathic abilities. Remote viewing too."

Maz, with all the spin and hyperbole of a seasoned cabinet minister, added a vague but intriguing follow-up statement: "The more things he tries the more we discover he can do. At the moment we're still exploring exactly what he is capable of. He's like a bottomless well of miracles." He looked extremely pleased with himself for coming up with this catchy impromptu sound byte. "There's your headline ladies and gents of Her Maj's press!"

A well-known face from lighter BBC television news reports asked if there was any truth in the persistent rumour that Serghei had been part of a Russian military research programme. That rumour had of course been anonymously leaked to the press by Maz, right after Serghei's triumphant appearance on *The Jonathan Ross Show.*

Serghei, with an inscrutable look, gave his well-rehearsed response, "I am not permitted to talk about that. I am sorry."

The young female journalist got a chuckle by chipping in, "Presumably that means you were!"

Maz added further to the mystery with a consciously ambiguous, "It means he can't talk about it. Sorry, darling."

A slightly more hard-bitten, middle-aged male TV journalist from ITN pointed out that there were sceptics who were saying that all Serghei's so-called paranormal demonstrations were merely magic tricks.

For the first time Serghei looked a little uncomfortable and hesitated. Maz quickly jumped in, saving the day with his cheeky banter: "And there are people out there who still think the Earth is flat, the moon's made of cream cheese and Victoria Beckham can actually sing. We respect everybody's right to be wrong every now and then. And make a complete arse of themselves!"

The chuckle round the room appeared to show that he had successfully deflected the inevitable, but awkward question.

The ITN man unfortunately persisted, however, by asking if Serghei would be willing to have his powers tested under laboratory conditions by scientific experts, to prove the sceptics wrong.

Serghei bristled at this. "I don't have to prove anything to anybody."

Maz recognised that sulky expression and knew he had to intervene again before his tetchy acolyte lost the crowd. "Serghei doesn't have to prove anything, but he has nothing to hide either, so if scientific experts choose to test him then of course we will cooperate. Any other questions?" Maz looked out into the room, as far from the ITN man as possible, for a change of subject.

To Maz's relief a fresh-faced young reporter from an obscure local paper enquired what the very first paranormal thing was that Serghei could remember doing.

Back on track Serghei relaxed. "It's hard to remember because everything seemed perfectly normal to me. I do remember when I was playing with toy cars, I suppose I was maybe four or five, that they used to move without me pushing them, but I just thought everybody could do that. It was other kids at school that first tell me I was different."

The cub reporter seemed delighted with this answer, and asked where Serghei thought those powers came from.

With absolute conviction Serghei said, "From God, of course."

That simple statement caused quite a furore with cameras repeatedly flashing again and excitable journalists talking over one another.

The next morning Maz and Serghei were back in Maz's club with a new stack of newspapers on the bar between them, plus an open bottle of house Champagne and two glasses. It wasn't really Champagne, as it came from Bulgaria, but that's what the girls called it in front of the punters, to justify the price tag of seventy-five pounds a bottle. It was perhaps a little early for bubbly, but they had a lot to celebrate in Maz's eyes. The place wasn't yet open, but it was noisy with a delivery of bottled beer being shunted on trolleys into the stockroom behind the bar, and the clinking empties going in the opposite direction.

Despite the fact that all the papers were carrying positive stories and features, Serghei was, as usual, grumbling. He was demanding to know why Maz had so readily agreed for him to be tested under laboratory conditions.

"Because I know you can fool them."

"Easy for you to say," groused Serghei.

Maz genuinely did have faith in his ungrateful discovery. "Look – everybody is so desperate to believe in you they'll be a push-over. And once you've been validated by a couple of crackpot gullible scientists with their endorsement, there really is no limit to how far we can go with this.

Hey – did you like the way I spun it so that the ones who don't believe in you are the nut-jobs and the loonies?"

Serghei thawed a little at the memories of the many good moments from his first ever press call. "The Russian military programme seemed to go down well."

Maz grinned, "And we never said that was real. I love the way they fill in the blanks for us. That story will just grow and grow, and we don't have to say another fucking word on the matter." Maz topped up Serghei's glass. "Here's to you my son!"

They chugged their so-called Champagne in a moment of silent jubilation, then Maz grinned. "You know the thing that really amuses me? All these hard-nosed investigative journalists firing searching questions at you, and not one of them asks the really big question…"

"What's that?"

"Well, if God really had singled you out and given you miraculous powers, why didn't he give you something a bit handy like the power to raise the dead, or turn cat turds into gold nuggets? Why the hell would he think it would benefit mankind to bestow upon you the power to mentally mutilate perfectly good cutlery? Still – fuck 'em! They are the ones who are going to make you rich beyond your wildest dreams."

Serghei raised an eyebrow. "You think?"

"I don't think. I know! The timing is just perfect. When there's a recession, and we're all feeling the pinch, the great unwashed look for something to cling on to. Give 'em a bit of hope. Trust me. The world was waiting just for you…"

* * *

Clive was sitting watching *Loose Women* on television, when the door opened and in bustled his mother with her morning shopping. She pointedly dropped a copy of *The Daily Mail* onto the sofa, next to him. The banner headline said it all: 'A bottomless well of miracles'.

"Your Russian friend is on the front page of all the papers again this morning."

"He isn't Russian, and he most definitely is not my friend!" snapped Clive.

Molly tutted disapprovingly and suggested 'the green-eyed monster' was rearing its ugly head again, which of course Clive vehemently denied.

"Anyway, turns out you were wrong about him," Molly continued. "He really has got powers of the mind."

"Says who?"

"*The Daily Mail*. See for yourself," she said, pushing the newspaper towards her son.

"But that's just what he's told them to say!"

Clive threw up his arms in exasperation. "I give up!"

Molly continued to suggest that Clive was jealous of Serghei's success.

"I am most certainly not jealous. It's just that I don't like him taking advantage of people's gullibility; deceiving them; preying on their hopes and fears."

Molly looked aghast. "What on Earth is wrong with giving people hope?"

"Nothing whatsoever. It's false hope I object to."

"I don't understand you sometimes," his mother said, shaking her head, "I really don't."

"I'll expose him for the charlatan he is, then you'll see. I'm not letting him get away with this!" fumed Clive.

The rules of engagement were beginning to fall into place. Could Clive be the one to bring Maz and Serghei's impressively tall but flimsy house of cards crashing down around them, or was he about to take on a dangerous foe he couldn't possibly beat?

CHAPTER SIX

Serghei had a grim expression on his face as he loaded the gun. Slowly and methodically he slid five empty bullet cases and one single live bullet into the six chambers of the hand revolver. He then spun the cylinder several times before slamming it back into place with the familiar metallic clunk heard in countless Hollywood westerns. In this context it was a much more chilling sound.

Slowly and dramatically Serghei hooked his finger around the trigger and raised the gun. His hand was trembling slightly as he put the cold barrel against his own right temple. The audience gasped, almost as one.

The eerily silent television studio was in darkness, apart from two stark spotlights picking out Serghei and a distant whiteboard with a heavy white balloon hanging in front of it. The live TV close-up revealed a shiny patina of nervous sweat on Serghei's forehead. He was breathing hard, almost hyperventilating. He closed his eyes, held his breath and mouthed a silent prayer to himself. Suddenly, startling the studio audience, he yelled loudly before squeezing the trigger six times in quick succession. There were three rapid clicks, then he suddenly pointed the gun at the balloon for the fourth 'shot'. There was a terrifyingly loud bang as the gun fired and the balloon exploded, splattering fake blood all over the whiteboard and the studio floor. Without missing a beat Serghei pointed the gun back at his own head for the final two fast empty clicks.

A good proportion of the audience screamed at the painfully loud gunshot, but they all erupted into wild cheers and applause as Serghei allowed the smoking gun to drop to the floor, letting out a huge sigh of relief, half bowing, half stumbling forward, as though he might faint.

For added dramatic tension the whole one-hour Serghei 'special' had been broadcast live, and this was the breathtaking climax. The audience at home breathed again as the credits rolled, signalling the end of the programme, relieved that they hadn't witnessed the nation's new golden boy blowing his brains out live on TV.

Foolhardy maybe, but these were the kind of stunts which were to add to the mystique surrounding Serghei, and cement his universal reputation and fame.

The next morning all the tabloid newspapers had plastered the story of Serghei's controversial and reckless PK experiment with Russian Roulette all over their front pages.

Maz, mobile phone in hand, was wandering around his empty lap dancing club, fielding the calls and complaints with undisguised glee. Caroline Stead, Head of Programmes at Channel Four, was telling him that his boy had got them in trouble last night, with seven hundred and thirty-eight complaints, and counting.

Maz, with his usual lairy attitude, didn't seem overly concerned. "Yeh, well it would have killed the drama stone dead if he'd turned to the camera and said, 'Don't try this at home, folks!' And somehow, with Russian Roulette, it doesn't feel terribly necessary."

Caroline laughed warmly, "Don't worry about it…"

"I wasn't," Maz grunted, in all honesty.

"I know how these things go," Caroline continued. "By close of play today we'll have had another five hundred complaints from people who didn't even see it. Publicly we are being very contrite and apologetic. Privately the management are doing cartwheels up and down the boardroom. It's the first time one of our programmes has made front-page headlines since we pissed the Queen off ten years ago!"

"We're not apologising, sweetheart!" Maz said bluntly, turning to a young delivery guy and bawling, "Not there you brainless twat! Round the back! Jesus!" He then carried on talking to Caroline, as though nothing had happened. "Look, if it sparks a load of copycat revolver-owning maniacs to give it a go – one in six of 'em deserves to splatter his fucking brains up the wallpaper!"

The TV executive winced, but couldn't help applauding the black humour. "Please tell me that's not your official press statement!" she laughed. "Seriously though, Maz, what will you say to journalists?"

"Not a lot," he shrugged. "Serghei's limited grasp of Her Maj's English doesn't run to the word 'sorry'. Trust me – I speak from bitter experience. He'll give 'em one of his enigmatic moody silences, which work remarkably well when he can't think of anything to say, and I'll just take the piss!"

Both parties knew full well that the complaints and media furore would make the viewing figures even higher for the scheduled late-night repeat in three days' time.

History records that around twenty magicians have died over the years performing illusions with guns, particularly during The Golden Age of Magic, in the late nineteenth and early twentieth centuries. Major theatres would dedicate themselves to staging spectacular shows, starring magicians like Maskelyne, Devant and Houdini, who were the rock stars of their day. During that period Serghei's version of Russian Roulette would have been regarded as a showstopping, but dangerous trick that few would have even attempted. Since then safer methods have been devised and magic props are better engineered and more high-tech, so the odds of survival were very much in his favour. The sceptics questioned what Serghei's stunt had to do with paranormal powers, but the spin for the media was that, through psychokinesis, Serghei had willed the only real bullet in the six revolver chambers to stop in the fourth position when he spAn the gun cylinder. Gun experts couldn't disprove this version of events, so the public became even more convinced of his God-given paranormal gift.

Exactly as Maz had planned, there was a frenzy of media interest, with ever-increasing offers from all the major television companies. They had put together a touring theatre show, which was an instant sell-out wherever it went. Tickets were like gold dust. It was a licence to print money. The people of Britain wanted to see this miracle-worker in the flesh. Cash was pouring in faster than either Maz or Serghei could possibly spend it, so financial advisers were quickly employed to stop it all going to the taxman. Serghei soon forgot his reticence about pretending his magic was 'real'. This kind of fame and fortune would never have come to a mere magician, however good he was with a pack of cards.

Neither he nor Maz had any conscience about their deceit, because, at this stage, it was only about entertainment, so what harm were they doing? It was a welcome distraction for the public and the media, and a money-spinner for them, just like any other superficial celebrity story. Win, win!

* * *

In the untidy editor's office of one the major British tabloids, Lindsey Montgomery, a young reporter, was looking over her boss's shoulder at a mocked-up headline on his computer screen. It read: *'Serghei Mystifies Scientists'*.

She raised her eyes to heaven. "You're not seriously going to run with that nonsense about him having God-given powers, are you?"

"Why not? The great unwashed are lapping it up," Derek, the somewhat jaded, balding editor, replied, with an equal lack of conscience to that of Maz and Serghei.

Derek Hyland had employed Lindsey straight from university. Right from her first interview he saw in her the hunger and the investigative desire for exposing truths, lies and humbug that he'd had at her age, which had gradually been beaten out of him by the system, and the necessary compromises to climb the ladder of success in a partisan corporate business. She was feisty and occasionally disrespectful, but he secretly admired that in her. He knew she had the makings of a great journalist. Unfortunately, great journalists are often wasted on tabloid newspapers. Lindsey was a perceptive young woman and could see that her boss must have once had the same fire in his belly that she felt, and she found it frustrating that he appeared to have surrendered.

"But his superhuman claims have to be total bollocks, right?" she said rhetorically, with the certainty and freedom of youth.

Derek shrugged and made the unarguable point that Serghei had indeed managed to convince a bunch of scientists, under laboratory conditions, that he wasn't using trickery, so who was he to argue.

"Was this before or after their mid-morning whiff of giggling gas?" Lindsey disdainfully enquired.

"You be as cynical as you like," Derek said firmly, "but I am running with the story."

Lindsey stood her ground and said that she wasn't being cynical, just enquiringly sceptical, which is surely what he was paying her for. Derek gently reminded her that ultimately they were all being paid to toe the party line by Sir George, their demanding proprietor. He then terminated the discussion, but not before having the last word on the matter. "Call your attitude to Serghei what you will, but while he's selling newspapers, and in the process keeping us all in work, don't forget, I'm more than happy to print that he's hearing 'the word of God'…"

'The word of God' was a slight exaggeration, but Serghei was hearing the word of a man who was perhaps beginning to think he was God. In the touring theatre show Maz could secretly speak to Serghei, while he was on stage, from a microphone in the locked dressing-room, his voice being picked up by a tiny invisible earpiece.

One of the highlights of Serghei's performance involved him reading the minds of genuinely random members of the audience. The person would covertly write a name, a word, a phrase, or a place on a clipboard, which nobody could see. Serghei would then concentrate hard, stumble around for a few moments to add to the tension, as though he wasn't sure, then suddenly would announce the correct word or words. The person would then show the clipboard to the audience as confirmation that Serghei had indeed read their mind.

In actual fact, Maz had read their handwriting. The clipboard concealed a meticulously designed electronic pressure pad which transmitted every movement of the pen to a laptop computer in the dressing-room. All Maz had to do was read out whatever had just been written to Serghei on stage. The ingenious props were being custom-made by a magical supplier in Japan, and shipped to an anonymous-sounding Stanley Masters, to avoid any links to Serghei.

On the first night they did this theatrical 'mind-reading experiment' a woman had written the word 'Bangkok' on the clipboard, which Maz was instantly able to read and transmit to Serghei, through his earpiece. He then floundered around a little, for dramatic effect, building to a big announcement:

"Oh, this is a place… A place a long way away… East… Very east… Far East… Is your place in Thailand maybe? … Bangkok!"

The woman visibly lit up, turning her clipboard round to show to her neighbours in the audience that she had indeed written the word 'Bangkok'. Of course the audience applauded appreciatively, but Serghei could milk more out of the revelation:

"I don't need to ask if I was right – your mind was shouting it at me. Yelling Bangkok."

Maz murmured into Serghei's ear, "Scary hole Bangkok! There's only three reasons people go there – a donkey-shagging show, one off the wrist from a lady-boy, or a dodgy watch."

Serghei did a quick mental edit for appropriateness before repeating the notion to his audience. "The only reason people go to Bangkok is for a sex show or a cheap watch," he said with a smile. "Does the watch keep good time?" Of course when the woman said she didn't buy a watch he was ready to counter with, "Well I hope you enjoyed the show."

These kind of Maz-prompted ad libs received a great reaction from the audience.

It felt good to get the odd laugh from the crowd, but, after the first couple of nights, they shrewdly changed things up, having discovered that this 'mind-reading' display had an even greater impact if there was some strong emotional resonance to the words chosen by the random audience volunteers. Serghei would ensure that any chosen name was the name of somebody recently departed, or any chosen place was somewhere of heartfelt significance, or the word or phrase was highly personal in some way. The audience member would tug at the heartstrings by telling their emotional story, without giving away the words or name, so that Serghei could claim that their subconscious was transmitting that deeply-held thought to his own finely-tuned and receptive mind. This guaranteed that the audience reaction was even more rapturous.

The whole show was imaginatively packaged, and cunningly put together. From the theatre seating-plan and the online booking records they knew the names and addresses of most of the audience, and where they would be sitting. The day before each performance they would go on social media and search for a handful of interesting audience members, who give away surprising amounts of personal information about themselves online. While Serghei was on stage the next night Maz could read to him from their copious notes:

"Look for a blonde woman in the left stalls, either seat D11 or D12. She's called Alicia, she's got a spaniel called Sunny, and her dad's in hospital, nothing too serious. Tell her he'll be home soon. That'll get a round of applause, and she might cry. She and Georgie, her daughter, went to Disney in Florida back at Easter, and they just did a sponsored run dressed as characters from *Frozen*. It was for Macmillan Nurses, because Alicia's mum died from cancer last year."

The people involved were frequently reduced to tears by the uncannily accurate revelations, and audiences were blown away by their reactions.

Serghei would also run through his tried and tested 'experiments' with PK. He would bend spoons and keys, stop watches, explode lightbulbs, move inanimate objects. He didn't reprise his Russian Roulette, however. That genuinely did have a risk factor, and was safer left as a memorable television one-off.

Audiences were always invited to bring along watches that had stopped working. They were told to stick them in their pocket or handbag. After dramatically stopping somebody's wristwatch on stage Serghei would announce that he was about to use his powers to do the reverse. He would raise his arms messianically and stare out into the audience, murmuring over and over, "Work, work, work, work…" The entire audience was then asked to delve into their handbags and pockets for any broken watches they had brought along. It was an absolute guarantee that the change in temperature, or vibrations from movement, would have made at least a couple of watches start ticking again, even if it was only for a few minutes. The owners would shout out and triumphantly hold up their watches, to have their own moment in the spotlight. That's all it needed for Serghei to take the credit, to tumultuous applause.

Everywhere they went they left behind awestruck audiences, many of whom had been genuinely moved by the experience, not to mention bins full of mangled cutlery and broken lightbulbs. The whole Serghei phenomenon simply grew and grew, beyond anybody's wildest dreams, as did his and Maz's bank accounts.

CHAPTER SEVEN

Clive and his mum were sitting watching *Celebrity Family Fortunes* on television when the doorbell rang. A hungry Clive hurried to the door, eagerly anticipating the takeaway he had ordered forty minutes earlier. He couldn't unchain the door to their flat fast enough.

"That smells good! I'm starving!" he enthused to the weary-looking Asian delivery man, who was standing there with the large paper carrier bag full of fragrant Indian food. "How much do I owe you?"

The bored delivery man told him the total was twenty-one pounds and fifty pence, and imparted the welcome news that the package included two free popadoms as it was over twenty pounds. Clive rubbed his hands together and asked the man to wait while he raided the Quality Street tin near the door, where their housekeeping ready cash was kept. Clive opened the lid and looked in, suddenly registering horror and swearing loudly. He dashed back to the door and asked if the man could take a credit card. The poor chap just looked to heaven and sighed.

"Give me a minute. I can phone through to the shop with my credit card details," Clive pleaded.

"No credit card. Cash only. They tell you on the phone when you make order!"

Clive, in a state of near panic, started rummaging through his pockets. He produced a ten pound note and a couple of small coins. He then spotted his mother's purse and found a couple of pound coins.

"I've got just over twelve quid. Can you leave the korma and the onion bhajis, and one pilau rice? That's about twelve…"

"Don't order from us again, please!" snapped the delivery

man, turning on his heels and walking off with the meal, muttering 'wanker' loudly under his breath.

An aghast Clive went back into the room and started berating his mother. "That was embarrassing! Thanks for that! I put fifty quid in there yesterday."

"I was going to put it back tomorrow, when I get my pension," Molly bleated.

Clive didn't need to ask what she'd spent the money on.

Molly defended her impulsive spending by reminding Clive how good Cecil Goodchild was as a spirit medium.

"He's a great comfort to me. He even told me where Don and I went on our honeymoon!"

Clive nearly exploded. "You already know where you went on your honeymoon! You've spent fifty quid of my money on finding out something you already knew! Money well spent I'd say. Meanwhile I'm bloody starving."

"You don't understand. He had a message from Don."

Clive told his mum, in no uncertain terms, that she was dead right he didn't understand. He didn't understand how she could be so bloody gullible.

Ten minutes later, his anorak collar turned up against the driving rain, Clive despondently stood at the cash machine, taking out a single note, and walking with it to the nearby gaudily-lit kebab shop.

* * *

The very next day, dressed in matching bespoke white tuxedos, Maz and Serghei were quaffing the finest Champagne as they patiently waited for Simona to enter the lavishly decorated country house hotel function room in her floor-length designer wedding gown. She looked stunning as she made her entrance, with her pretty Russian dancer friend, Nadia, alongside as her only bridesmaid.

Nadia worked for Maz in the club, so she knew him well, and you know what they say about the best man and the bridesmaid, so it promised to be a fun occasion.

The four of them giggled their way through the whole ceremony, much to the registrar's benign bewilderment. They were still giggling as they signed the wedding register. They felt they had a million reasons to celebrate and be happy.

When the official proceedings were final, and the registrar had made her excuses and fled, Maz said they should just step out into the hotel grounds for ten minutes to 'get a few photographs', which he'd arranged. That was the first time Serghei stopped giggling. As they emerged from the stately baronial hall entrance they were confronted by a veritable army of paparazzi, journalists, press photographers and TV news cameramen. Far more than the select few Maz had invited, to be honest, but word had inevitably got around.

Despite his immediate anger Serghei managed to force a smile for the cameras, but hissed under his breath, "What the fuck are they doing here?"

Like a ventriloquist, his lips barely moving as the cameras relentlessly flashed, Maz murmured, "Keeping you on the front pages, my son, and thereby helping to maintain the rock 'n' roll lifestyle to which you are rapidly becoming accustomed."

With that essential but irritating chore reluctantly suffered, Serghei quickly forgot all about it, and went back to enjoying himself as the celebrations continued privately indoors. Their Champagne bill alone would have exceeded the cost of most wedding receptions for a hundred guests.

There was little point for speeches, but Maz did manage to slur an inebriated toast to the not-so-blushing bride. "I wanted to give Tiffany, sorry, 'Simona', away today, but she's never given herself away – she always charged a fucking fortune. I was going to say 'an arm and a leg', but you could get a helluva lot more than that, if you were prepared to haggle."

Even Serghei managed to laugh, albeit through slightly gritted teeth, as Maz continued, "So I'm best man instead. Best man by far, some would say. Anyway here's to gaining a client-in-law, but losing a bleedin' good pole dancer. Bottoms up, sweetheart!"

The wedding was yet another instance of the familiar pattern which was beginning to emerge, whereby Serghei believed he was getting all his own way, while being blissfully unaware that he was being manipulated. He had been perfectly content simply cohabiting with Simona, but she had quietly been watching the money come rolling in. During one of their many rows about her job, she had made it clear that if he put a ring on her finger, making her financially secure, then she would agree to stop work.

Much has been said over the years about the romance of marriages made in heaven, but it's probably fair to say that the jury is still out on a marriage made in a lap dancing club.

* * *

Like most people Clive Entwhistle was unaware that Serghei's secret wedding was even taking place, not that he would have cared. At the time of the actual vows he was in his bedroom, all four walls adorned with eye-catching Victorian magic posters, busy at his laptop updating his Facebook page. He looked very pleased with himself as he sat back and re-read his latest posts. He was a man on a mission.

The next afternoon he was sitting watching *Pointless* on television, when in bustled his mother with his older, married sister, Sarah. Molly had a radiant glow about her. Clive acknowledged them both, but didn't get up. Molly took off her coat, asking Clive if he wanted a cup of tea as she was about to make one for Sarah before she headed home. Clive declined as he'd still got a cold coffee sitting on the folding TV dinner table next to him.

His mum then turned to Clive and said, "I know you won't ask, but Cecil was brilliant today. Sarah will tell you. You won't have it, but he's so gifted." She then disappeared into the kitchen.

The moment Molly was out of earshot Sarah sat next to Clive and, with undisguised irritation, asked why he couldn't be a bit more supportive. He told her that he couldn't possibly be supportive over that crooked charlatan that their mother insisted on seeing.

Sarah tutted and said, "You should encourage her to get some comfort and solace from her visits with him. It's closure for her."

Clive was livid. "Yeh, well it's alright for you to breeze in here once a month, when it suits you, laying down the law about what's good for her and what isn't. You've got some neck to tell me how to deal with her! I'm here every day and, yes, I hate her seeing that swindling bastard!"

Sarah was unmoved. "He's really good, as it goes. She believes in him. I've seen it for myself. He says stuff he couldn't know if he was a fraud. He got her wedding day to Don dead right, and knew all about his crown green bowling. You're just tight about her spending the money. She told me."

Clive was almost rendered speechless by the unjustness of the remark. He managed to rail against the unfairness, more frustrated than angry, because he knew he was right, and would soon be able to prove it. "That is so not fair! It breaks my bloody heart to see her being taken in, if you really want to know."

"Now, now. What's this? Raised voices? That will never do. What's been going on?" Molly chided, walking back into the room with a mug of tea for her daughter.

"Oh it's nothing, Mum," Sarah said in a soothing voice. "Just something on telly last night. You know what he's like. Always knows best."

"Oh don't I just know it!" Molly cooed, patting Clive's face in a patronising way, before pulling the free newspaper out of her bag and dropping it on the sofa next to Clive. "Here, I brought you this."

The headline read 'Mystic gets hitched', with a photo of Serghei's wedding day.

Molly stated the obvious, "Look here. Your Russian friend's only gone and got his-self married. Bonny girl too."

Clive petulantly threw the newspaper back at her, declaring, for the last time, that Serghei was not his friend, and pointing out that his bonny bride was in fact a stripper, hoping his mother would be shocked.

Molly suggested that perhaps he should have made more of an effort to be Serghei's friend, as he was so successful now.

That was the final straw. Clive demanded that they change the subject, then, fearing that they wouldn't, he stormed off to his bedroom.

"Ooh, somebody's touchy today!" crowed his big sister.

CHAPTER EIGHT

In an exclusive cocktail bar, within a renowned five star Mayfair hotel, two men were sitting watching the uniformed waiter fussing with their drinks, coasters and ramekins of upmarket nibbles. It was obvious they didn't want to speak in his presence. Both men were smartly dressed. They had to be to get in through the door. However, one of the men, Keith Taplow, was in an expensive Savile Row pin-striped suit, and wearing a significant school tie over his hand-stitched shirt, whereas the other, Johnnie Collins, was more 'man at Primark', adorned with nearly as much bling as Maz Masters. It was inescapable that the men came from very different social standings. Public school versus the school of hard knocks. The cocktail waiter was serving Keith with a large single malt Scotch and soda in a squat cut-glass tumbler, and Johnnie a bottle of over-priced Czech lager in something which resembled a slender vase.

When, at last, they were alone they resumed their conversation in hushed tones, which seemed to be tinged with suppressed menace.

"I trust we can expect a good turn-out for the march on Saturday?" asked Keith rhetorically.

"Have I ever let you down?" Johnnie asked, equally rhetorically.

"Your usual motley mob of tattooed, brick-throwing, Neanderthal knuckle-draggers, I assume?"

"Yeh, well, Pippa Middleton and Tim Rice had prior engagements."

"Point taken," nodded Keith, taking an appreciative sip of the smooth golden liquid. There was a moment's silence, then he began again, "There was another reason I wanted to see you."

"I guessed it wasn't just for a pickled egg and a pint. Go on…"

"What do you know about this 'Serghei' fellow, who's all over the front pages at the moment?" asked Keith, stroking his left earlobe between thumb and forefinger.

"Haven't given 'im a lot of thought to be honest. Just another 'ere today, gone tomorrow fairground sideshow freak."

"Don't be so sure. There has been some very clever marketing. They are no longer putting him out there simply as an entertainer. He's started doing day-long seminars on life skills and personal development. Total bollocks of course, but he feels like a quick fix for the disenfranchised. They're paying upwards of three hundred pounds just to listen to his self-help platitudes. Lapping him up they are. I'm not sure anybody has quite spotted what they've got there."

It was true that Maz had indeed persuaded Serghei to read everything they could find on self-help and positivity, so that he could cash in on his burgeoning fame as a 'mystical guru', and go out holding life-coaching events up and down the country. People were mesmerised by his words and going away empowered and buzzing with joie de vivre. And it was easier than coming up with a new full programme of magic tricks which could be passed off as paranormal experiments.

Keith Taplow added darkly, "I'd like to meet him…"

* * *

Home from honeymoon, and newly ensconced in her marital home, a much more exclusive ultramodern apartment in a gated community, Serghei's bride was wandering around aimlessly, trying to readjust to her newfound life of leisure. She was almost relieved to hear the gate call-bell sound. It was Maz, so she pressed the appropriate buttons to allow him access to the complex. When she opened the apartment door Maz sauntered in, without invitation, as though he owned the place.

"So, how was the honeymoon, Mrs Iliescu?" he asked,

cheekily squeezing her left buttock as she led the way to the kitchen. Simona smacked his hand away, not hard, but firmly enough that he got the message.

With a smile, but an equally firm tone, she said, "I don't work for you no more. A kick in the balls is suddenly an option."

Maz looked suitably chastened, not to mention disappointed. "Sorry, sweetheart. Force of habit."

With the new ground rules established, Simona happily answered his question, "Honeymoon was reassuringly expensive. Very nice. First time first-class on plane. I never see cabin crew smile before."

"So his passport worked okay?" asked Maz. "It's amazing what you can get down the East End when you've got a few quid. Where is he?"

Simona explained that Serghei was with someone, but wouldn't be too long, so she offered Maz a tea or a coffee while he waited.

"As a hand-job appears to be out of the question, I suppose I'll have to make do with a cup of builder's. Thank you, darling."

Simona was still finding her way round their new-fangled kitchen, and was searching everywhere for the kettle, before she remembered that boiling water came out of a special chrome tap, on demand. Movement could be heard elsewhere in the spacious apartment, then muted voices. Maz craned round to see who was out in the hallway, heading for the door. He was shocked to see Serghei ushering out a woman and a child. The deathly-pale, sickly-looking youngster had no hair, and was wearing a plastic tube wrapped around his face and under his nose, attached to a portable oxygen tank, which his mother was carrying. Even for somebody as hard-bitten as Maz they made a distressing sight. He stood, turned and watched in horror as the tearful woman left with a grateful farewell, almost curtseying to Serghei as she guided her little boy out through the door. Maz was aghast. The moment the door closed he sprinted over to Serghei, angrily demanding, "What the fuck was that?"

"Just trying to help. Y'know, like I give something back."

"You're doing healing?" Maz roared. "Have you gone out of your tiny Romanian mind? You're a fucking conjuror! Or had you forgotten?! I don't mind you conning dumb adults with a few harmless tricks, but what you just did is fucking sick!"

Serghei looked a little uncomfortable, but defended himself. "I'm not doing no harm, and his mother says it is helping."

Revealing a hard side the newly-weds had never seen before, Maz really lost it and grabbed Serghei by the throat, pinning him against the wall. "Not doing any harm? You've completely lost the frigging plot, haven't you? We made it up that you're some new fucking Messiah, you arsehole! It's not real. You're just a two-bit illegal immigrant trickster! Don't ever admit it, but don't you ever forget it either. This stops – right now. No more! You hear me?"

Maz let Serghei go, then brushed himself down, trying to get his thoughts together. "Are they due again?"

"Next week," Serghei said sheepishly.

"You cancel! I don't care what you tell them, just cancel. Tell them to listen to his doctor – poor little bastard. But if you see him again I swear I'll personally expose you for the fucking fake that you are!"

* * *

Lindsey Montgomery was writing a front-page piece on Saturday's anti-austerity march, which had turned ugly, marred by scenes of violence and mindless vandalism. She was under the watchful eye of her editor, Derek Hyland, as this was a major story and, as such, the tone had to be in line with their proprietor's somewhat reactionary views. On a personal level Lindsey had been sympathetic with the march, agreeing that some of the draconian austerity measures supported by particular elements of the fractious and splintered Tory government were stacked against people who were already poor and needy. She also felt that the admittedly shocking disorder had probably been created by a handful of rent-a-mob troublemakers, bussed in to take credibility away from the thousands of well-meaning people who wanted to make their feelings known to an out-of-touch government which was refusing to listen. Of course that wasn't the angle Hyland wanted for the front page of his right-wing rag. He was almost salivating over a snatched close-up of a tattooed thug's nasty expression as he lashed out at a policeman with a wooden bat. That was the photograph he wanted everybody to see, whether it was truly representative of the day or not.

"That's much better," he said, as he made her delete the somewhat staid photo of the massive march snaking its way through central London.

Lindsey frowned and shook her head. "Doesn't it kind of miss the whole point of the march, and the predominantly well-intentioned people who went on it?"

"Ah! Integrity. I remember that," Derek intoned wistfully. "Trouble is earnest lefties don't sell papers. Trust me. Middle England loves nothing better than feeling superior to ugly, mindlessly violent protesters. I can almost hear them tutting over their muesli and poached eggs as we speak."

Knowing she wasn't going to win on such a political battleground, Lindsey decided to negotiate instead, suggesting to Derek that, as he got his own way on this one, then perhaps he would let her do a piece on Serghei.

"Don't let this genial exterior fool you. I'm not running a democracy here. It's a not-necessarily-benign dictatorship. What is it with you and this Serghei anyway?" he asked.

"Nothing," Lindsey lied. "Well, not really. It's just the whole phenomenon around him, the way it's escalating. It's kind of disturbing, I suppose."

"Oh, alright," sighed Derek. "Do a profile for next Saturday if you must. But a positive human piece. Lots of pictures of him and his foxy wife looking fabulous. Take him out to lunch, ask him about his honeymoon, and God…" Then, almost as an afterthought, "And get him to bend you a spoon."

In the end Lindsey was frustrated. It wasn't the piece she had wanted to write, questioning Serghei's authenticity and putting the acceptance of his so-called 'powers of the mind' under the microscope. In fact, she found herself having to do the complete opposite, giving his whole publicity machine yet more oxygen. Meeting him though confirmed her steely resolve. She could see right through his attempts to charm her with his obvious sexual magnetism. She disliked sexually aggressive men, and she wasn't impressed by his unsubtle evaluation of her body when she introduced herself, or his somewhat dated flirtatious comments. There was no doubt that he was easy on the eye, but she found his predatory demeanour a complete turn-off.

Maz had engineered for Lindsey to attend a studio recording they were doing for a new television special. He made sure that he chaperoned her at all times, so that he could deflect any difficult questions and monitor exactly what she was extracting from Serghei. The time pressures in the studio also provided Maz with an easy get-out if he wanted to spirit Serghei away, thereby putting a stop to any interview topic he didn't much like. He had no reason to be especially suspicious of Lindsey. Maz was suspicious of everybody.

Lindsey found Maz vaguely amusing with his Jack-the-lad brashness, but she could see that he was clearly the brains behind the operation. It didn't take a genius to see that Serghei was no Einstein, despite his undeniable skills, or talents, or whatever they were. Much to her own annoyance though Lindsey had to admit that he did exude an aura of mystery and was infuriatingly charismatic. Together, there was no doubt that the two men made an imposing team.

The photographer assigned to her feature arrived during the meal break, as pre-arranged, and took a variety of moody shots of Serghei, plus some glamorous snaps of him with Simona, who was looking stunning, as always. At Derek's insistence there was even the obligatory shot of Serghei, one eyebrow mysteriously raised, looking over a bent spoon. This was definitely not the feature Lindsey had hoped to write.

She stayed for the recording of the show and watched the audience from the side. They were clearly enrapt by Serghei, all getting to their feet when he made his first appearance in front of them, a cheer almost lifting the studio roof. The receptive crowd were equally captivated by his 'paranormal experiments', which did indeed appear to defy scientific logic.

A well-known female science presenter was called upon to examine a large sealed Perspex box which contained two Perspex plinths, one of which bore a fifty-pound note, and the other an inert lightbulb with no holder or wires attached. Having declared the box to be impenetrable the celebrity umpire stepped aside to allow Serghei to move forward and psyche himself up, before staring intently into the box, waving his hands over the top of it. He started incanting undecipherable words as tense music built to an ear-splitting crescendo. Slowly the fifty-pound note started to rise, then gently spin in mid-air, illuminated by an ever-increasing glow from the disconnected lightbulb. When the light became so bright that the bulb popped and extinguished itself, Serghei staggered backwards melodramatically, as though himself burnt out, just like the lightbulb. Of course the audience were back on their feet, cheering and applauding this apparent miracle. Serghei was unsmiling as he bowed, but very obviously wallowing in their adoration.

Lindsey was still convinced that it was trickery, even though she could offer no obvious explanation herself. What she couldn't deny, however, was the innate showmanship and the crowd-pleasing allusion towards mysticism.

She was annoyed to admit it, even to herself, but she could see why the public were so in Serghei's thrall.

It wasn't just Lindsey's newspaper who were happily and willingly giving Serghei free publicity, rapidly making this self-professed new messiah the most talked about person in the land. Glossy celebrity magazines were paying fortunes for 'at-home' features with him and Simona. Every tabloid paper boasted photographs of Serghei posing with rock stars, the beleaguered Prime Minister and minor Royalty. Major corporations were jumping on the PR bandwagon, with headlines about an international petrol giant recruiting Serghei, and paying him a million pounds, to help them find new oil and gas reserves. As usual Serghei couldn't lose. They were taking him to an area known to be rich in fossil fuels anyway, so the odds were in his favour. If, by chance, he found anything it guaranteed both him and the oil company another day of newspaper headlines, and, if he failed, his employers were bound to hush it up, to avoid looking like gullible suckers. Which ever way the headlines went it was certainly better PR than Greta Thunberg was giving them.

Even the England football team were photographed with Serghei at Wembley, after he had managed to take the credit for an almost dead cert cup win, with the headline: *Serghei's powers ensure England victory against Germany.*

CHAPTER NINE

After numerous visits Molly Hill had just about exhausted every beyond-death possibility with Cecil Goodchild, the ageing spirit medium. Nevertheless, he had fed her addiction for communicating with her late husband Don, so she was continuing to spread her spiritual wings and was attending her second séance with a younger and more dynamic medium, Dominic Powers.

Molly had saved hard to see him a few weeks before and couldn't wait to relive the experience, despite the quite exorbitant cost. Mr Powers had made several appearances on morning television, and so his services were considerably more expensive than Cecil's, thanks to his 'celebrity' status.

He made the effort to look the part as well, sitting at the head of the table with his bleached highlights, bleached teeth, and pumpkin-hued fake tan. His professional premises were more stylishly modern than Cecil's, but with a nod to the classic candlelit eerie ambiance his fee-paying clients expected. Sort of gothic Ikea.

Molly's daughter Sarah was allowed to impassively observe for an extra thirty-five pounds, so she sat back and watched the six women, of a certain age, join hands around the table. The wall lights dramatically dimmed as they did so.

Powers spoke with a clipped sibilant voice, and a curious turn of phrase. "Let's see who's out there," he said, closing his eyes. "Advance spirit friends. Commune with us from the spirit world, and move among us. Oh! I have somebody coming in already, thank you please. It's a man. Lovely, lovely man. Deary-lord preserve us! What is he doing? He's putting a cigarette out in a drink." Powers suddenly cowered and flinched, "Oh my days! He's smashed the glass! Somebody understands that, don't they please?"

"It's my Michael," one woman said in a hushed emotional tone.

"That's right it is. Thank you, Michael," he said, repeating the name in order to usurp the credit for knowing it. "Michael is saying he should have done that many many moons ago. The doctor did warn him, didn't he, thank you?"

"Time and time again," sobbed the woman.

"But he ignored the warnings. He has a message for you, but, oh! Wait! Don's here, Molly! Michael says he doesn't mind waiting, thank you please."

Molly looked positively radiant and sat up.

"Don's whistling something, Molly. What's that you're whistling, Don? Does he have a favourite tune, Molly?"

"It'll be 'The Last Waltz'," said Molly, grinning from ear to ear. "He always said that were 'our song'. He never were much of a whistler, mind, but he were always humming."

Impressively quick on the uptake, a skill perfected over several years, Dominic started humming 'The Last Waltz' to himself, as though he'd been humming it all along.

"That's it," cooed Molly. "Ah, bless 'im…"

"Don's talking about Paignton, near Torquay. You understand that don't you, Molly, thank you please?"

"You went there together!" chimed in Sarah, so impressed by the fey medium's apparent insight that she was unable to contain herself.

"That's right. Just before he passed over," quavered Molly.

"The Esplanade, please?" Dominic continued, ever-more confidently.

Molly was overcome. "Oh fancy 'im remembering the hotel!"

The medium was on a roll. "I feel like it's Christmas, but it's not Christmas, is it, Molly? You understand that don't you please?"

Molly nodded emotionally, "*Tinsel & Turkey* they called it…"

"It's sad, really," Sarah said, helping her tearful mother out, and of course unwittingly helping Dominic out at the same time. "It was one of those hotels where they do Christmas every week. The doctor had said Don might not make it to Christmas."

"Which he didn't," sniffled Molly.

"So it was a way for them to have one last Christmas together."

"Ah, bless you both," Dominic intoned. "Don says Christmas Day and Boxing Day every Saturday and Sunday from September to January."

Molly sobbed at the memory. "That's it."

"You enjoyed it, didn't you? One last Christmas before Don's sad passing." Dominic was consciously milking her emotion. "Oh, Don's laughing now. I don't understand it. He's saying something about baked beans and a black bird. Do you understand that please?"

Molly managed a smile through her tears. "It made him laugh. A mynah bird it was. In the hotel dining room. In a cage. At breakfast the woman there used to ask if you wanted beans, and the mynah bird always said 'Stinker, stinker! Don't have the beans!' It were ever so funny."

"Yes, Don's laughing. He's also talking about a big clear dome. And a forest, like a jungle, please?"

Molly suddenly looked puzzled. "I don't understand."

"Don says the coach tour took you on from Paignton to see the Eden Project in Cornwall. The indoor rainforest experience."

Molly's expression changed. "No, that's not right. We come straight 'ome. Don was too poorly to go any further. I've never been to Cornwall."

Dominic, feeling his powers mysteriously ebbing away, quickly changed the subject. "Oh, Don says he's pleased you're redecorating the bedroom. It's time to move on, he says. He thinks the pink flowers will look lovely when it's all finished, thank you. You understand that Molly, don't you please?" His tone was beginning to sound a little desperate.

Molly became upset again, but for a different reason. "No.

Tell 'im I'd never change our bedroom! I don't know where he got that idea. It'll always be just as it were when he was with me…"

* * *

Clive Entwhistle was sitting watching *Tipping Point* on television when he heard the door open. He had his laptop next to him, ready for the almost inevitable denouement which was about to unfold. His mother and Sarah, his older sister, walked in silently, looking a little forlorn, and certainly not as full of themselves as they had been last time they returned from a séance with TV's Dominic Powers. Clive turned down the volume on the television and asked the glum pair how it had gone.

Sarah shook her head, scowling, "Oh today he takes an interest!"

"I can't win," said Clive. "If I don't ask I'm in trouble. If I do ask I'm in trouble. Damned if I do, damned if I don't. I presume it didn't go too well today."

"He just had a bit of an off-day, that's all," Molly sighed, taking off her coat.

Sarah was trying to buoy her mother's spirits. "He got some things right".

"Let me use my psychic powers," Clive said, making cod mystical gestures in the air and putting his fingers to his temples. "I'll bet he told you that you visited the Eden Project in Cornwall and that you are decorating your bedroom with pink flowers."

Molly looked at her son in disbelief.

"How the hell did you know that?" snapped his sister.

"Oooohh. I'm a psychic too!" Clive answered, rather too smugly.

"Stop it, Clive!" his mother implored. "I don't understand."

This was the moment Clive had been waiting for. "As I've said all along he's a fraud. They go online, find the family connections and look at everybody's social media. Your Mr Powers has been looking at my Facebook page."

Clive picked up his laptop and read his most recent post from the screen, "I have to get into the Christmas spirit today, which is a bit weird at this time of year. Doing magic for 'The Esplanade' in Paignton…" Clive turned the screen for them to see. "Look – I even found a nice photo of the hotel." Turning the screen back he carried on reading, "… Doing magic for 'The Esplanade' in Paignton, where they do Christmas every weekend. Mum and Don went just before he died and they loved it. They kept going on about the funny mynah bird in the dining-room. They went on to the Eden Project afterwards and were blown away by that, but I'm coming straight home. I have to finish decorating Mum's room. I think she'll like it when it's all done, but the pink flowers seem a bit over the top for my taste."

"How could you?" demanded Sarah, angrily.

Clive looked shocked. "How could I what? All I did was make up some nonsense on my own personal Facebook page. I wasn't the one who tried to pass it off as a message from the other side!"

"Alright, smartarse!" snarled his sister. "How do you explain him knowing all about Don's crown green bowling last time we went? He was real specific about that."

"Let me read you my Facebook entry from four weeks ago." Clive scrolled back on the screen of his laptop and started reading again, "Mum keeps trying to persuade me to join the bowling club at Blackheath, just because Don was a big noise down there, but it's an old man's game. No way am I even tempted." He sat back, with a self-satisfied look.

Sarah wasn't giving in, however. "But Dominic knew that Don had been Vice President and won cups".

"Yeh, well, frauds are sneaky. There are only two bowling clubs in Blackheath. He phones them up, posing as a long-lost friend, and asks about Don. Simple as…"

In fact, Dominic Powers had done no such thing. He was

far too busy and important. There was also every chance his distinctive voice would be recognised. However, his young under-paid researcher had phoned both clubs to find out more about the late Don Hill and his impressive bowling record. The same diligent young researcher who, four weeks later, phoned the Esplanade hotel in Paignton to enquire about their *Tinsel & Turkey* weekends, and ask what the story was with the funny mynah bird he'd heard so much about.

Molly looked completely bewildered. "I never tried to talk you into joining Don's bowling club," she said, missing the point completely.

Clive had been so single-minded about exposing this confidence trickster that he hadn't really stopped to think about the devastating effect his revelations were going to have on his mother. Poor Molly slumped into her armchair, tears rolling down her cheeks, looking as though her whole world had just collapsed around her.

"Satisfied now?" snapped his sister, putting a comforting arm around her mother and glaring at Clive.

Dominic Powers and Cecil Goodchild had conned his mother out of money she could ill afford, and filled her head with false hope, yet somehow Clive had ended up the villain. As Plato once said, 'No one is more hated than he who speaks the truth'.

CHAPTER TEN

As usual, in daylight, Maz's lap dancing club looked seedy and in urgent need of decoration. A cruel-looking, tattooed man with an ostentatiously prominent gold front tooth was loudly haranguing a harassed barman.

"Have you got the new price list programmed into the till yet? And why haven't you got all those fucking crates in? What the fuck have you been doing all morning, yer lazy turd?"

An attractive, but unfashionably dressed young raven-haired woman cautiously entered from the street, uncertain of these clearly unfamiliar and quite daunting surroundings. Unsure of herself she inched forwards and approached the shouting man.

In broken English she hesitantly enquired in a strong Eastern European accent, "Excuse please. I am, er, look for…"

The man shamelessly looked her up and down and interrupted, "Not bad. Not half bad, babe. Good legs, nice tits. Where have you worked before, darling? Turn round, let's have a look at yer arse."

The young woman looked a little unnerved, to say the least. "I don't look for job. I come look for Mister Masters. Private matter."

"He's not 'ere any more, darling. Sold out. I'm the guv'nor now."

The woman looked deflated. She had obviously just reached a highly unwelcome brick wall at the end of a long and arduous search.

"You know where I, er, find Mister Masters?" she asked lamely.

"How should I frigging know? I'm not running the Tourist Information, sweetheart."

With that he callously turned his back on the crestfallen woman and walked away to find somebody else to shout at. Looking downcast and helpless she turned to leave. Fortunately, Candy, one of the dancers, spotted her. She was casually dressed, having just arrived, but was heavily made-up, ready for work.

"You looking for Maz, babe?" Candy enquired. "Flash git's moved into some fancy-arsed office block in Wardour Street. You'll find it easy enough. Smug twat'll have his name in letters six foot high."

The foreign woman looked grateful, yet bewildered. It was obvious she didn't have a clue where Wardour Street was, and didn't have sufficient English to comprehend anything Candy was talking about.

The dancer took pity on the lost looking woman. "Look, I get it. Me and him have history." She took out her smartphone and scanned through her long list of contacts, then scribbled something on the back of her raunchy private business card, handing it to the stranger, speaking slowly and deliberately, as only British people can to both small children and foreigners. "Show this to a cabbie. Taxi driver. Black taxi cab. It's Maz's new address. Mr Masters. Don't tell 'im I give it yer. Good luck, babe."

The young woman took the card, thanking Candy profusely, and turned to leave.

The new manager called after her, "If you change your mind about a job darling, this place could do with a girl with big tits and a bit of class!"

"Fucking charming!" yelled Candy, sticking up her middle finger at her new boss, knowing full well he needed her more than she needed him.

The 'fancy-arsed Wardour Street office block' was indeed ultra-modern and rather opulent looking, all glass, chrome and marble. It was a multi-purpose office complex, shared by several affluent companies who wanted to impress visitors and clients. A uniformed commissionaire welcomed the raven-haired young woman through the silent automatically-opening doors and ushered her to the main reception desk. She was told that, unfortunately, Mr Masters wasn't in his office at the present time, and the crisply-dressed receptionist didn't know what time he would be back, advising her to make an appointment.

The stranger had come too far and got too close to give up, so, rather than leave, she slipped over to the busy waiting area, sat down and feigned great interest in the marketing and PR magazines which were fanned out across the large glass-topped table. She wasn't quite sure what she was planning to do, and she didn't know what Maz looked like, but she instinctively felt she stood more chance of speaking to him so long as she remained inside that building.

Over an hour passed. Dozens of people came and went. The burly commissionaire was beginning to take an interest in the lingering presence of the oddly-dressed stranger, when suddenly the doors glided open and a flashy looking man in a camel-coloured cashmere trench coat swaggered in, calling out to the attractive receptionist, with a wink, "Hi there, Ali! Alright, darling?"

The girl on the desk smiled dutifully and called back, "Hi Mr Masters. I'm good. You?"

The stranger's ears pricked up, hearing the man's name. Quickly she hurried over to intercept him before he disappeared towards the bank of lifts.

"Mr Masters. I need speak with you."

Maz looked uncharacteristically flustered and tried to side-step the woman who was blocking his path. He obviously wasn't accustomed to being door-stepped in his new high-rent environment.

"I'm so sorry, Mr Masters," called out Alison, the receptionist. "I did tell her that she'd have to make an appointment."

"Very important, please. I want talk with you about Serghei Iliescu," the stranger pleaded.

It wasn't often Maz Masters' blood ran cold, but it did on this occasion. So few people knew Serghei's family name. Ever since his protégé's meteoric rise to fame Maz had been half expecting the dreaded tap on the shoulder. Somehow though this woman didn't look like an immigration official. But then what did an immigration official look like? He did think it would be ironic, but not impossible, for an immigration official to speak in such broken English. All sorts of things were going through his mind. Surely immigration officials hunt in packs. Somehow he felt she wasn't bringing glad tidings, whoever she was, so he took her firmly by the arm and manoeuvred her into a corner, away from prying ears.

"Who are you?" he asked. "Are you from…? Are you here in an official capacity?"

"No, no. Private matter," the stranger said, much to Maz's relief.

"It's just that not too many people know his surname, never mind pronounce it properly. Well, if you're just a fan, darling, leave your address with Alison on reception, and we'll make sure you get a signed photo."

"I am not fan. Most certainly not fan!" the stranger said emphatically. "It is very opposite in fact. My name is Aurelia. I come all way from Romania. I am Serghei's wife."

Maz could not have been more taken aback if a small nuclear bomb had detonated just outside the door.

A couple of hours later Maz was sitting on the expensive white leather corner sofa in the newly-weds' apartment, glaring angrily at Serghei. He wanted to shout and bawl, but he had to keep his voice down as Simona was just through next door, in the kitchen. Anxiously Maz kept a watchful eye on the door in case she walked in. He almost spat out his whispered words, he was so incensed.

"You didn't think to mention to your Best Man, before he bought you a very pricey non-returnable wedding gift, that you were already bleedin' married?"

Serghei was, for obvious reasons, equally anxious about

Simona overhearing and kept glancing towards the kitchen. "That was in a different life. We were young. Too young."

"But there never was a divorce?"

"Not as such."

"That'll be a 'no' then!" Maz gasped in exasperation.

"Anyway," Serghei said defensively, "that was Romania. This is UK."

"That's not how it works!" snarled Maz. "You can't have a wife in every frigging country! Jesus Christ – you'd have fifty-four just in Africa! You'd never afford the anniversary cards."

Serghei looked quite offended. "Some time you talk to me like I'm a fucking idiot."

"There's a very good reason for that, my friend!" snapped Maz, before stopping to think.

At that moment the worst happened and Simona did breeze in from the kitchen. She couldn't help but notice how the conversation abruptly stopped and she was greeted by an awkward stony silence.

"What is going on?" she asked.

"Oh just old Mystic Meg here," sighed Maz. "Always full of surprises."

Serghei shot Maz a look, which Simona couldn't fail to see. She looked from one man to the other with increasing suspicion.

In a serious tone which Simona recognised, from her days as an employee, Maz asked if she'd give them a minute, as there was boring business stuff to sort out. Reluctantly she turned on her heels and went back into the kitchen.

"Aurelia just want money, as usual," Serghei said, shaking his head, as though his Romanian wife was in the wrong somehow.

"You bet your arse she wants money. A shit-load! Worse than that though, she wants your bollocks. Her fifteen minutes in the fucking spotlight." Maz pushed back his hair and sighed, getting himself back under control. "Look. I've moved her out of the mingin' B&B she'd checked herself into, holed her up in a nice hotel instead and given 'er some spenders to splash in Knightsbridge. Give us time to think."

"You let her stay?" Serghei gasped, raising his eyebrows. "Why you not send her home?"

Maz looked despairing. "For a so-called fucking visionary you sometimes can't see past your own bleedin' nose, can you?"

Despite the fact that this was all his own doing, Serghei sulked.

CHAPTER ELEVEN

Lindsey Montgomery was sitting at her computer in the newspaper office, taking advantage of a few quiet minutes at the end of a busy day to do some research, more for her own curiosity than anything. As frequently happens when you search on the internet, one thing leads to another. Not for the first time she searched for 'Serghei', and was overwhelmed by the thousands of results the great God Google offered her. You would have thought there had never been another soul called Serghei in the history of the planet. His Wikipedia page described him as a psychic entertainer. That led Lindsey to Google 'psychic', then 'medium' and 'clairvoyant', but that was taking her off-topic. 'Psychic fraud' provided some interesting links, which she followed with fascination. Adding the word 'exposing' to her search delivered yet more results. When she then added 'Serghei' to the mix she stumbled across a link to a YouTube clip of a magician who claimed to expose psychic frauds. The clip had already been viewed and 'liked' several hundred times.

Lindsey wandered over to the communal coffee machine and poured herself a cup, then returned to her desk, rummaging in her drawer for her headphones, which she plugged into the computer. Sipping her hot black coffee, she sat back and clicked 'play' on the magician's latest YouTube offering. The earnest young bespectacled man was sitting in what looked like his bedroom, surrounded by gorgeously evocative Victorian magic posters. The rookie reporter smiled at his mundane moniker, Clive Entwhistle, a name not exactly sparkling with showbiz glitter. He did speak with great passion though, so she listened as he addressed the laptop camera in front of him.

"Welcome to my vlog. The great Harry Houdini, probably

the most famous magician of all time, spent the last few years of his life exposing fraudulent mediums and debunking fake séances. He abhorred the use of trickery to profit from people's grief. My own mother has been such a victim, seduced by fake messages from the other side, delivered by a supposed clairvoyant, or spirit medium, or whatever he calls himself, Dominic Powers. Who better than a magician to see beyond the smoke and mirrors of trickery and scams? I have followed Houdini's lead. As my followers will know, I have already revealed Mr Powers' fraudulent techniques in previous clips, which are still available to view. Please share this link with everybody you know so that we can expose more of these charlatans who cynically prey on the needy and grief-stricken."

Lindsey's ears then pricked up as, with undisguised bitterness, Clive continued his diatribe:

"I also intend to expose the new darling of the media, sham guru and would-be psychic Serghei, who is himself no more than a good close-up magician. Remember – the bigger they are the harder they fall! I'm Clive Entwhistle. Thank you for watching."

Lindsey took off her headphones and scratched her head, thinking. She carefully bookmarked the link to Clive's YouTube channel before shutting down her computer for the night.

* * *

Wonderland was a busy bar in a fashionable part of central London. It was always packed with journalists, lawyers and trendy television types, so it was a pretty noisy environment, full of empty chatter. Lindsey and Clive, both with glasses of red wine in their hands, moved away from the bar and found a small table, facing one another. They said 'cheers', chinked glasses and took a sip of their drinks. Conversation was slightly stilted at first.

"Sorry about that," Lindsey started. "I was at the other end of the bar and I didn't see you standing there."

"And I didn't know what you looked like," said Clive.

"No, of course not."

"No problem though. I've only been here ten or fifteen minutes."

Lindsey apologised again and Clive reassured her that he really hadn't minded waiting. There was an awkward pause so they both took another sip of wine.

As the person who had instigated the meeting, Lindsey felt obliged to break the ice, so she suddenly said enthusiastically, "So – you're a magician?"

"Yes, for my sins," smiled Clive.

"Show me a trick!"

Clive visibly brightened. Like all good magicians he had a pack of cards ready in his jacket pocket, and, also like all good magicians, he didn't need asking twice. Clive fanned the cards out, face down, in front of Lindsey and invited her to pick a card. She slid one out and looked at it, covertly.

"Not the Jack of Diamonds. That makes it too easy," said Clive, with a smug smirk.

Lindsey grinned from ear to ear, throwing down the Jack of Diamonds.

"How on Earth did you know I'd pick that, damn you? Are they all the Jack of Diamonds?"

"Oh, so journalists are all as cynical as they say," smiled Clive. "No. They are all different. Look." He turned the cards over to show they were indeed a normal pack. "Put your card back into the middle of the deck."

Clive offered her half the deck, so she obediently picked up her chosen card and placed it face down on top. Clive then slapped the other half of the deck on to Lindsey's card, which was still protruding from the middle. He even turned the deck over to show that it was indeed her Jack that was sticking out from the centre. He then squared the deck up, did an impressive riffle shuffle and placed the cards down on the table.

"I said put it in the middle, not on the top."

Lindsey looked quizzical, but dutifully turned over the top

card, only to find it was of course her Jack of Diamonds. She clapped enthusiastically, much to Clive's obvious delight. She couldn't resist picking up the other cards to inspect them herself, but they were all different as he had promised.

"You're right," grinned Lindsey. "Working for a newspaper does make you cynical."

"Alright. I'll give you another chance. I'll make it easy for you," Clive said, very deliberately sliding her card into the centre of the deck and giving them a thorough shuffle. He then gave the cards to Lindsey, asking her to spread them out on the table, face up, and see where her card was now. The young journalist pushed the cards around the table, separating them with her right forefinger, but completely failed to find her chosen card. The Jack of Diamonds had vanished completely.

In a somewhat confused voice she said, "It's not there!"

With that she looked up at Clive, only to find that he was sitting there with the Jack of Diamonds stuck to his forehead. Lindsey laughed appreciatively.

"Very good!" She clapped again.

Clive, looking pleased with himself, peeled the card off his forehead, gathered up the rest of the cards and slipped them back into his jacket pocket. Lindsey was so gushingly impressed he began to think he might be in with a chance. In fact, she was way out of his league, and she only had one possible intention in mind regarding this tentative meeting with Clive, and it certainly wasn't romance. Lindsey sensed the magician's animal aspirations, but didn't want to encourage him, so she changed her body language accordingly. She rather regretted wearing a short skirt. It was force of habit when she was interviewing the male of the species. Men were so transparent. Cynically she knew she would always get them to say more than they really intended.

With the flurry of excitement and easier chat regarding Clive's impressive card tricks set aside, the atmosphere became stilted again and they both sipped their wine, with Lindsey tugging her skirt hem as close to her knees as it would go.

After a pregnant pause she decided to avoid any misunderstandings and cut to the chase, telling Clive how she found his YouTube channel interesting, especially his latest vlog entry.

"Thank you," he said. "It's just the beginning really. Is that why you wanted to meet up? It would be great to get some national newspaper coverage for my campaign. Maybe we can work together on exposing frauds?"

Lindsey asked Clive if he had confronted Dominic Powers and exposed him publicly. The magician had to admit he hadn't been that audacious.

"That would have been more of a story," said the journalist bluntly. "Does he even know you debunked his techniques?"

"I can't be certain, but I'm sure it got back to him."

Lindsey was unimpressed. "It's not much of a story. Psychic hears on the grapevine that he's been caught cheating."

The stinging reprimand made Clive feel rather foolish, so he descended into another awkward silence. Lindsey took a sly glance at her watch, beginning to wonder if she was wasting her precious time. She knocked back most of her wine, preparing for a quick get-away.

Lindsey broke the hushed stalemate again with one last attempt. "So what about this Serghei then? I gather you're not a fan?"

Clive instantly took the bait and snapped into gear, taking off vocally on his favourite hobbyhorse. "That charlatan! I cannot believe how people can be so gullible! Ninety per cent of the population have been taken in by this claptrap that he's actually got God-given powers! Ninety-nine-point-nine per cent probably! It's unreal!"

Lindsey suddenly became interested again in her nerdy new ally. "And you don't think he has got mystical powers?"

"Of course he hasn't! He's a magician, just like me. All his so-called miracles are just tricks. I can replicate anything he can do."

"You can?" Lindsey asked, her interest peaked. "If that's

true he somehow managed to fool the experts."

"They should have had a magician there. I know him. Knew him. He's a con man, a two-bit hustler!"

Lindsey nodded. "I interviewed him for a feature and he readily admits that he had to scratch a living on the streets before he was discovered."

Clive was beginning to sound more and more bitter. "Right. And does he 'readily admit' that he used to steal from his clients?" He paused for a non-existent reply. "No! I thought not!"

Lindsey downed the rest of her drink, suddenly riveted by Clive's vitriol. "Let me buy you another one. In fact, why don't I get a bottle?"

CHAPTER TWELVE

In an exclusive dark oak-panelled dining room, within a renowned five-star Mayfair hotel, an unholy trinity had gathered for the first time. Seated around a vintage red leather-upholstered private dining booth, Keith Taplow and his sidekick Johnnie Collins were sandwiching Serghei in between them. They were all smiles, already inebriated, as the young French sommelier skilfully popped the cork of yet another bottle of vintage Champagne, offering to top up their cut-glass flutes. Keith told him to leave it, saying he'd do the honours. The sommelier smiled and took away the empty bottle, lovingly nestling the new one into the ice bucket before he left them in peace.

"I'm so sorry, Serghei. Where are my manners?" Taplow said. "Would you rather finish on cognac or port? They have a particularly fine vintage port here."

"No, no. This is fine. Very good," Serghei said, draining his glass for his host to top up.

As he poured, Keith asked Serghei if he had enjoyed his evening. After such a gourmet fine-dining feast and so much exorbitantly-priced booze it would have been churlish to say no.

"You would love the boat. You must come down to Monte Carlo for a couple of days," Keith said, before turning to Collins. "He'd enjoy the boat, wouldn't he, Johnnie?"

"What's not to like?" the hardman nodded, betraying no real emotion.

"Simona. My wife. She would like that I'm sure," agreed Serghei.

"Oh, well now," Keith confided knowingly. "It's more of a

stag really." He could see that Serghei looked puzzled. "A little break from our good ladies, if you see what I mean."

With a sly humourless grin Collins elaborated. "Bit of quality time with a few bad ladies for a change, if you get our drift."

Serghei nodded slowly, mulling over the intriguing prospect in his mind.

"Not your thing, Serghei?" enquired Keith obligingly, before leaning in closer. "What's your preference? We can cater for most tastes."

"No, the stag boat, it sounds good. Very good," nodded Serghei.

"To Monte Carlo!" toasted Keith, raising his replenished glass.

The three men all chinked their glasses together and echoed the toast.

Taplow glanced at his watch and then nodded furtively towards Johnnie's phone, which was sitting on the table next to Collins.

Like any good trickster, Serghei didn't miss a thing and reacted to his host looking at his watch. "I guess I should be going home. Thank you for most good evening, gentlemen."

"No need to venture out into the cold, dear boy," urged Keith. "We thought you might like to make a night of it."

As he said this, Johnnie Collins was sending a text: *Your on girlz!!*

"We've booked you into the Presidential Suite," continued Keith.

"I don't know," said Serghei, stroking his chin. "I say I'd be home."

"Ah, what it is to be young and in love," smiled Keith. "You've got a phone haven't you? Let the good lady know you'll see her in the morning."

Serghei was protesting that it was late to call Simona, when he spotted the two sexily-clad, high-class escorts who were shimmying towards their booth.

"You'll like it here," winked Collins. "We've even got

someone to tuck you in."

"Good evening, ladies," Keith oozed, not allowing Serghei chance to argue. "Would you care to show our guest to his room?" With that he handed the tall blonde a gold key card.

"Ooh! The Presidential Suite!" she squealed. "Big bed in there! Plenty of room for three!"

Serghei simply couldn't resist as she invitingly held her hand out to lead him away. Collins stood up to let him out. As the men shuffled positions the petite redhead started taking the Champagne bottle from the ice bucket.

In a colder and harder voice than he'd used all evening, Taplow stopped her. "Leave that, sweetheart! There are a couple of bottles in the fridge. Phone room service if you need any more."

Keith and Johnnie smirked as they watched the expert girls link arms with Serghei and lead him off. Collins looked positively envious, but Taplow had a more measured expression which simply said 'job well done'.

Smugly, Keith raised his glass again, as soon as they were safely out of earshot. "To Serghei! God-given powers or not, he was certainly sent from heaven."

"I still don't get it," sighed Collins. "What do we need with his load of old pony?"

"You really don't get it, do you, Johnnie, old boy? He's already become a guru, worshipped by all and sundry. With the right people pulling the strings he could be the next sodding Messiah. Look, we've got a quarter of the voters behind us and another quarter tempted by us, but only one fucking seat in the Commons. With the right figurehead we could change the political landscape for ever. No more two-party system." Then he paused and added darkly, "No more elections…"

"But he's not even a politician," Collins unnecessarily pointed out.

"Oh right, because the great unwashed love politicians so much. Don't you see? That's his appeal."

Johnnie nodded, seeing the undeniable logic behind Keith's

thinking, then looked up and asked, "What about Rupert?"

"He served a purpose. Very useful in the early days, all that blokey, beer-swilling, everyman charm. But I have enough dirt on him to have him quietly retiring to spend more time with his family whenever I snap my fingers." Keith savoured his Champagne, then carried on, almost as though he was thinking out loud. "Change of party name too, I think. Something more worthy sounding. Spiritual even."

Collins looked shocked. "It's taken us years to get the name out there."

"It's just a bloody name. It didn't harm sales when Marathon bars became Snickers. And they still have just as many nuts."

Keith topped up their glasses before checking one last all-important detail. "I take it you are making a little keepsake of tonight? They always come in handy sooner or later."

Sure enough all three strategically hidden miniature cameras were recording everything in the Presidential Suite. It was all going to be there for posterity. Either posterity or blackmail, but posterity wasn't such an ugly word. The movement sensors had been triggered the moment the threesome tumbled drunkenly in through the vast suite's double doors, capturing the two giggling escorts stripping Serghei naked as they staggered their way to the massive Emperor-size bed, peeling off their own clothes in the process. Even more damning was the carefully stage-managed appearance of the cocaine from the tall blonde's Gucci handbag, which Serghei, with very little encouragement, proceeded to snort from the petite redhead's bare buttocks. A discreet veil should be drawn over what happened next, but, suffice to say, it was precisely what Keith Taplow wanted to have on record. Just in case it was ever required.

* * *

At ten o'clock the next morning an unusually rattled Maz turned up at Serghei's apartment, uninvited, wanting an urgent summit meeting to discuss the Aurelia problem. He had learned the code to allow him access to the secure gated community, so he was already standing outside the apartment door, pressing their buzzer repeatedly. Simona opened up. As usual Maz barged in like he owned the place.

"Where the hell is he?" he demanded, looking round.

Simona pulled her dressing-gown around her. "And good morning to you! He not here, as it goes."

"Has he just told you to say that? Is he hiding in the bedroom? I really need to see him sweetheart, right now. No messing."

"I tell you, he is not here!" Simona insisted, looking nearly as rattled as Maz appeared to be. "And if he was here, he dead, because I kill him!"

"So where the fuck is he? He's not answering his phone."

Simona glared at Maz, undaunted by his aggressive demeanour. "I was going to ask you same thing. I thought he is with you."

"I haven't seen him since the day before yesterday," snapped back Maz.

Fury was mounting in Simona's eyes. "He said it was business. After midnight he send text – *Don't wait up, kiss, kiss, kiss.* He kiss my ass!"

Slowly the penny began to drop. Maz knew that Serghei had received a clandestine invitation to dinner, so, putting two and two together, he guessed some temptation must have come along, and he knew all-too-well how weak his protégé was when it came to temptation. Quickly he back-pedalled, covering for Serghei. Things were bad enough already.

"Oh right, yes of course, I forgot. What am I like? There was a business thing in town last night. I told him to check into a hotel if it got late and he'd had a drink. My fault, babe."

Simona didn't look convinced. "You men stick together like legs of nun."

"Quaint expression you got there, Mrs I. No, honestly darling, it's me. I clean forgot."

Just then Maz was quite literally saved by the bell. The call-bell sounded from the gate, with somebody requesting access.

Simona flounced over to the telephone entry box on the wall, which allowed her to speak to the person outside. She pressed a button and sharply snapped into the oval microphone grille, "What you want?"

"Let's hope it's not Charles and Camilla popping round for tea and crumpets," mused Maz to nobody in particular.

A female voice crackled through the small speaker, "I need talk with Serghei Iliescu."

Maz recognised the accent immediately. His heart sank. He ran to the window and looked out. As he feared it was Aurelia standing by the large black gates. In desperation Maz dashed to the door to go outside and intercept her, repeating the 'F' word to himself, over and over as he ran.

"So do I babe! I need talk with him very bad!" snarled Simona into the telephone entry system. "But he's not here. Who in hell are you?"

"It very important," pleaded Aurelia, not knowing who she was speaking to.

"How you get this address?" demanded Simona.

"I follow Mr Masters. In taxi. I know him. He say two days ago I can speak with Serghei."

Maz had reached the gates by now, panting for breath. He pleaded with Aurelia through the cast iron bars. "This really isn't a good idea, darling."

Undaunted Aurelia continued to hold down the call button on the gate entry box, and spoke into the microphone once more, "Who are you? One of his girlfriend?"

Maz reached through the gates, with great urgency, and tried to pull Aurelia's finger off the silver button, to end the potentially explosive conversation. "Please, darling! This isn't the way!"

She fought back, slapping his hand away, "Sterge-o! Leave me!"

Simona's irate voice then came back through the speaker, "I'm his wife, babe! Who in fuck are you?"

Maz became frantic and scrabbled once more through the

gates to stop Aurelia re-pressing the communication button and replying. She was more than a match for him and bit his finger. Hard. Maz yelped and withdrew his hand, looking in horror at the bloody teeth marks. This gave Aurelia all the time she needed to press the nuclear button and say, "You not his wife! I his wife!"

Maz closed his eyes at the shocking revelation that could never be unheard, sucking on the painful bite, and gasped, "Oh Jesus Christ…"

CHAPTER THIRTEEN

In the untidy editor's office, a frustrated Lindsey Montgomery was standing in front of Derek Hyland's desk, hands on hips, pleading with her boss. Their expressions were akin to those of a long-married couple having a lively discussion about which programme they were going to watch live on TV – *The European Cup Final* or *Strictly Come Dancing*.

"Come on, Derek, let me run with this. I've made a great contact. A magician who says he can replicate all Serghei's so-called miracles with sleight of hand. He's a bit of a nerd, but he's a nerd on a mission. He exposes frauds. He exposed a fake medium, and now he wants to expose Serghei. He hates him. He knew him when he was a street hustler. Reckons he used to steal watches from the guests when he performed at parties. It's a great exclusive."

Hyland looked at his keen young acolyte wearily. "I let you do a puff-piece about him the other week. You did a good job. Nice human angle. But that's enough. What is it with you and this Serghei, anyway?"

"He's potentially dangerous. We should warn people."

"Dangerous?" Derek echoed, incredulously. "He's just yet another transient celebrity phenomenon. An overnight sensation. Next year it'll be a Royal engagement to a trans-sexual who was on *X Factor*. Or a cloned monkey who takes selfies and posts them on Instagram."

Lindsey shook her head, pleading her case passionately. "I think you underestimate him. There's something happening. Can't you sense it? It's scary. He's the new darling of the Royal Family; politicians are queuing up to be photographed with him, which is never a good sign; the big corporations are all desperate for him to endorse them. He's like bigger than Jesus all of a sudden. Doesn't that worry you? Because it frightens the bloody life out of me!"

Her editor pointed out that the Great British public can't get enough of Serghei, making him pretty much untouchable.

"Then surely it's our duty to put them straight!"

"Look, Lindsey," Hyland said, trying to put a swift end to an argument which his hierarchical position ensured he couldn't possible lose. "You've definitely got what it takes. You're good. I knew you would be. But you're still naïve. You'll learn."

"Don't patronise me!" Lindsey sighed.

"Is it patronising to share the scars of bitter experience? Maybe it is. But you have to just accept that some celebrities are Teflon. Indestructible. It was Jimmy Savile thirty years ago. We'd all heard the rumours, but not one newspaper dared touch him. He was a national treasure. Don't believe what all the righteous revisionists try to tell you. It's an uncomfortable truth now, but his big cigars, funny haircuts and eccentric antics sold papers, and his charity work made him so popular nobody would have wanted to hear anything bad about him, so we all left him alone."

Lindsey couldn't believe what she was hearing. "But don't you see that's exactly why I…"

Hyland was running out of patience and interrupted her, "Look I'm done with this petty obsession of yours. Just let it drop. I'm not letting you run with it. Sorry an' all that, but that's just the way it is. This paper is pro-Serghei, like it or not."

Lindsey snorted with frustration and stomped out of her boss's office, leaving him shaking his head.

* * *

That evening Lindsey and Clive were back in Wonderland. They were at the same table, and Lindsey was pouring full-bodied Argentinian Malbec from the bottle in front of them.

"Well there's good news and there's bad news," Lindsey sighed.

"I could use some good news," smiled Clive, whose mother still hadn't really forgiven him for the Dominic Powers debacle.

"I've started a blog about Serghei," said Lindsey. "Questioning his paranormal powers and suggesting that his rise to such massive fame, and the public adulation he's attracting, is not healthy. I've emailed you the link."

"Cool. I'll link to you from my YouTube page. So, what's the bad news?"

"Derek, my dinosaur editor, won't hear a bad word about Serghei, so he's refusing to run with the story."

Bitterly, Clive said, "He's got everybody eating out of the palm of his hand. I don't get it. It's unbelievable. He must be an intelligent bloke to be editor, surely?"

"You'd think, wouldn't you? Derek reckons Serghei's so popular right now he's untouchable. Compared him to Jimmy Savile, like that somehow explained everything."

A deflated silence fell upon the crusaders, so they sipped their pleasantly mouth-warming wine instead.

"I had another thought though," Lindsey said, brightening up. "I have a good contact on *Good Morning Britain*. Perhaps we should get ourselves on breakfast telly. They're always struggling for interesting guests who are prepared to get out of bed at that ungodly hour. The only downside is it might mean being interviewed by that well-known Alan Partridge tribute act, Richard Madeley..."

* * *

Less than half a mile away the other dynamic duo were having a quiet drink in Chico's, a much more exclusive private drinking club, frequented by celebrities and filthy rich business types. Maz and Serghei were looking intense and serious as the unsmiling waitress delivered their glasses of chilled Chablis.

When she'd gone Maz leaned in to talk discreetly. "Listen.

You're a bloody stupid arsehole. That goes without saying. But we are where we are, so we've just got to deal with it. We've both got too much invested in all this to let a minor 'domestic' bring it all crashing down. You get Simona back on side, and I'll take care of Aurelia. I'm not sure who's got the worse deal. Pity you go for these feisty sorts."

"How will you…?" Serghei didn't have the words, so pulled a face.

"I'm going to need quite a wad of cash from the business account. Don't worry. I'll find a way to claim it against tax."

"Sure," said Serghei bitterly. "She always like my money. But Aurelia is stubborn woman."

"Listen, my friend," Maz said, dropping his voice. "You don't run a lap dancing club in London for fifteen years without getting to know a few people who can be a bit convincing."

The truth was he didn't have the stomach for getting his own hands dirty, but he knew a couple of hired hands with much stronger stomachs.

Early the next morning Maz was carrying a small coral pink holdall as he walked out of the lift of a popular four-star Knightsbridge hotel and approached the reception desk.

"Good morning, sir. Can I help you?" asked one of the busy receptionists, in an accent which was hard to place.

"Just checking out on behalf of one of your guests, darling," Maz said, putting the plastic key card down in front of her. "She had to leave real early, for Heathrow. I'll settle her tab for her. Room 1076."

"That's not a problem, sir," the receptionist smiled, punching the keys of the keyboard in front of her, then looking at the screen. "Mrs Iliescu?"

"That's her," Maz said, taking out his wallet. "I'll settle the old-fashioned way. In folding ones. Cash, sweetheart. What's the damage?"

* * *

Gargantuan cranes were swinging, huge trucks and cement tankers were coming and going, and workmen were shouting over the noise of burrowing excavators on a massive industrial-scale building site in Croydon, just south of London. A new residential complex was being erected. A vast hopper was being navigated over a deeply-sunk walled shell to create a solid foundation for one of the buildings. A man in a hard hat and a high-vis jacket was shouting up to give the 'okay' to the hopper operator now that he was satisfied with its position. With a deafening noise, reminiscent of Niagara, cascades of liquid concrete came glooping out of the hopper, slowly but inexorably filling the empty shell.

What nobody noticed was the innocuous-looking muddy tarpaulin at the bottom of the shell which was quickly engulfed and entombed for ever by the thousands of gallons of lumpy grey gunk, as was Aurelia's limp lifeless body which lay underneath it.

CHAPTER FOURTEEN

It was 7am and Lindsey and Clive were sitting in the Green Room at the TV studio, from which ITV transmits *Good Morning Britain* live every day. They were both dressed to the nines for their big television debut together. Clive yawned loudly, unused to being expected to perform at this unearthly hour in the morning. The car which had picked him up had arrived at quarter past five. He had that peculiar heavy feeling in the pit of his stomach that comes with sleep deprivation. The nervous butterflies didn't help either.

The place was buzzing. Presenters, guests and weather forecasters kept coming and going every time there was a commercial break. Sound technicians were fitting people with personal microphones and earpieces; make-up artists were dusting everybody down to dull the shine of oily skin; sparky young researchers were checking everybody's stories and reminding them not to swear; and even younger trainees were plying everybody with strong coffee to wake them up and get their hearts kick-started.

"Nervous?" asked Lindsey.

"A bit," Clive confessed. "Don't worry though, I'll be fine."

"I'll get you to do a magic trick first. That always relaxes you."

Clive faintly smiled. "We won't be taken seriously if I sit there with a Jack of Diamonds stuck to my forehead."

"You do realise we are about to declare war here?" said Lindsey, more seriously. "He isn't going to take this lying down."

Clive nodded, "I know."

"He'll fight dirty. Like a cornered animal."

"What's the worst he can do?" shrugged Clive, positively relishing the battle ahead.

Despite all their misgivings about Serghei, it was impossible at this point for anybody to foresee the black-uniformed thugs who would form his unregulated armed militia in the not-too-distant future. This force would have alarmingly wide-ranging powers, their prime function being to keep order during the transition period into the new Greater Britain. Their unspoken secondary function, however, would be to silence all dissenters.

A fresh-faced smiling girl, wearing headphones and carrying a clipboard, approached Lindsey and Clive. "You'll be on in about nine minutes. Let's move to the studio so that the director knows you're ready. Sorry. No hot drinks in the studio."

"Is it too late to pay a last visit to the loo?" Clive asked.

"It is really, I'm afraid," the girl said, pulling a patronisingly sympathetic face. "Sorry about that. Let's go."

Coincidentally, Serghei was in front of television cameras on the same day, albeit at a much more civilised hour. So far he and Maz had managed to keep a lid on his self-inflicted domestic nightmare, so this was a major TV documentary profile on his life and career, including an in-depth 'at home' interview, conducted by one of the country's most popular television journalists, Dania Rhan.

Maz had wisely treated Simona and a couple of friends to a day of pampering and preening at a luxury spa retreat in the country, so she was safely out of the way. Their apartment seemed to be overrun by camera operators and technicians, running cables everywhere, erecting light stands and microphone booms, whilst others assembled camera tripods, which glided smoothly and silently along shiny black rail tracks.

Maz was pacing anxiously around, keeping a vigilant eye on the important proceedings. A make-up artist was fussing with Dania's long, luxurious, jet-black hair as the interviewer consulted the notes on her lap. Serghei was being fitted with a tiny microphone while the director talked to her camera crew about shots and angles. An obliging technician was rigging a small monitor for Maz, so that he could watch what was being recorded, and a sound engineer was asking if it was okay to turn off the air conditioning as he was picking up a low persistent hum.

Eventually the director seemed satisfied that they were all set to go and instructed everybody to stand by. Dania checked the hem of her skirt and smiled at Serghei reassuringly. "I'll do a bit of an introduction about you from the courtyard outside the apartment, so we'll just go straight into the interview, if that's okay with you."

"Nowhere that gives away the location, old love," Maz intervened. "He's already got more stalkers than Justin Bieber on a pub crawl in Romford."

Dania looked a little nonplussed, but the director assured Maz that they would find somewhere suitably anonymous and they would allow him and Serghei to approve the location.

"Alright, nice and quiet everybody, please," the director called out from her strategic vantage point, donning her headphones. "Run up to record."

The three camera operators pressed buttons, then clearly confirmed that their cameras were rolling and up to speed.

"And action!" called the director.

Dania cleared her throat, took a deep breath, looked up, smiled and began, "Before we start Serghei, can I just thank you for welcoming us into your home. I think people will be fascinated to see how you live. I have to confess it's not what I expected somehow. Very modern. I like it though."

"You are welcome," Serghei answered confidently. "I'm glad you like it."

"I imagined you in some dark rambling gothic mansion in the middle of nowhere."

"Maybe next year," Serghei smiled obligingly. "That would be nice, yes."

"The proceeds of the book should help," Dania said, picking up a hard-backed copy from the glass coffee table. "How does it feel to be a best-selling author now, on top of everything else?"

"It is very nice, of course," Serghei answered, a little at a loss for words.

Maz, who had deliberately positioned himself in Serghei's direct eyeline, gave him an encouraging look, urging him on.

"What is better is that I am helping people, I think," Serghei added, to Maz's nod of approval.

Dania glanced down at the book briefly. "I hardly need mention the title. It's already being reprinted, the demand has been so high."

"Go on. Force yourself!" Serghei said, sounding remarkably like his mentor.

Dania laughed, then turned to her dedicated camera. "Okay, well if you've been in a cave for the past couple of weeks, or on the moon, the title of Serghei's book is *ESP and the Power of Positive Thought*. I'd like to say 'available in all good bookshops', but it actually isn't just at the moment, is it? It sold out over the first few days. Over three quarters of a million copies."

"We did tell them to print more," Serghei said, shaking his head. "But it will be back in shops by the end of this week, I think. So they tell me."

Maz gave him a thumbs-up.

"They say the overnight queues outside bookshops even eclipsed the release of the last ever Harry Potter book," Dania gushed.

Serghei couldn't resist a self-satisfied smile. "So they say. It is very nice."

Ms Rhan put the book down and sat up, subconsciously checking her skirt hem again with her left hand. The obligatory contractual book plug out of the way, she assumed a more serious expression. "How exactly do you define ESP? Extra Sensory Perception?"

Pleasantries over, always a difficult area for Serghei, he happily launched into more familiar, comfortable and well-rehearsed territory. "For centuries now the human race has been blinkered. So-called experts talk about the five senses. It is ridiculous. There are six, seven, maybe more senses. Ancient civilisations knew these things. It seems we know less since we decide we know everything."

Dania checked him. "But not everybody can do what you can do, surely?"

"It is true that my powers of the mind seem to be more developed, and I would say that I have embraced that gift and harnessed the powers I have been given very well, but everybody is born with a certain degree of ESP. It is just we have been brainwashed into suppressing it."

"You did a fascinating experiment on television recently, to prove that fact. You secretly put three everyday objects into a locked and guarded bank vault safe, right?"

Serghei nodded, picking up the story. "And the viewers had to try to tune in to my thoughts, then write down what they believed I had put in that safe."

"The results were astonishing," Dania said. "A thousand or so got all three items right."

Maz shook his head frantically and held up his open hand, all four fingers and thumb outstretched.

Serghei picked up on the exaggerated prompt. "Five thousand by the time we check all the emails and texts. Over half a million viewers got at least one item right…"

* * *

Having been seen on *Good Morning Britain*, Lindsey had managed to get herself and Clive an audience with Rachel Rashford, a BBC television executive, who expressed interest in their crusade. They were sitting in Rachel's glass-walled Broadcasting House office, overlooked by a large photograph of Morecambe & Wise, viewing a recording of Dania Rhan's much-watched and critically-acclaimed profile on Serghei, which had been transmitted in prime time the previous evening.

When it came to the part about the ESP experiment with

the three objects in the safe, Lindsey couldn't help interjecting, "He just makes up those figures. Nobody ever questions them, and who's going to prove him wrong? It's unbelievable what people will fall for."

Clive picked up the mantle. "A load of people claim they get these things right anyway, even though they didn't. Because they want to kid themselves that they're special. That's how it works."

Rachel pressed the pause button and looked at the pair. "It's hardly Pulitzer Prize-winning journalism just to say 'liar, liar, pants on fire'…"

Lindsey wasn't giving up. "Clive can go on one of your shows and do all the things Serghei can do, by sleight of hand, which is a much cleverer way of saying exactly that."

Rachel sat back and pondered for a moment. "Then will you tell us how you did those tricks?"

"I can't reveal the methods, unfortunately," said Clive. "They'd kick me out of the Magic Circle. Magicians' Code an' all that, but I am happy to testify that they are all done using nothing but magician's trickery. No gift from God or mystical powers. And I'm less squeamish about calling Serghei a liar."

Rachel frowned. "You should be careful. He's becoming very litigious, apparently. And he can afford bloody good lawyers."

* * *

The morning after the triumphant Dania Rhan recording, his less-than-humble self-confidence boosted yet further, Serghei had been in a good mood. Aurelia seemed to have disappeared, for now at least, and he hoped Simona would be so relaxed, after her day of five-star pampering with her friends, that she might let him move out of the spare room, and back into the marital bed. He walked into the kitchen where Simona was arousingly dressed in little more than a striped shirt. She had her back to him, chopping fresh tropical fruit on the white marble worktop for her breakfast. Serghei crept up behind her and boldly slipped his arms around her waist, stroking her belly and nuzzling his head into her neck. Simona's right hand instinctively tightened around the handle of the sharp serrated fruit knife.

She froze, not physically responding to his advances, then said in a cold hard voice, "You have your secrets. There are also things you do not know about me. Punters in lap dance club like to touch, yes? We had contest to see which girl break most fingers. I won first prize every year."

Serghei wisely let go of her and backed off. "How long are you going to keep this up?"

"I haven't decided yet. How long are you going to keep being married to another woman?"

"I told you," Serghei pleaded, "she's history. That was another life. Trust me, she's gone. We'll never see her again."

"Trust you?" Simona snorted sarcastically. "This is good joke. Trust the man who has made himself rich and famous by lying through back teeth to whole country!"

"I don't know what you want me to say."

"I want you to say you divorce her. And I want to see papers to prove it."

"But she's back in Romania. Gone. We'll never hear from her no more."

Simona was unmoved. "When I see papers, then we get married again. Properly this time. Until we're married properly you're just punter."

She dropped the knife with a metallic clatter, pulled off her gold wedding ring and threw it at Serghei. "You need your fingers to do magic tricks, I think, so no touch!"

CHAPTER FIFTEEN

Sir George Henderson's sprawling Surrey mansion had its own banqueting hall with a ridiculously long dining table, which was always lavishly laid with starched linen, heavy silver, lead cut crystal and Royal Doulton porcelain, whenever there were guests in the house. On this occasion there were only four people seated around the table, but no expense had been spared. Sir George was naturally sitting at the head, in his antique oak carver. Keith Taplow and Johnnie Collins were sitting to his right, facing Maz Masters, who was still wondering what the hell he was doing there.

Two glamorously attired waitresses were in attendance. One was unobtrusively clearing away the small appetiser plates while the other expertly poured finest claret from a cut glass decanter.

Keith sipped the wine appreciatively. "So Mr Masters, how far are you planning to take it with your young charismatic protégé?"

Maz was guarded, to say the least. "I'm not sure I get your drift?"

"Well, is there an end game?" enquired Taplow.

"We're doing pretty well already, I'd say."

"Oh, so would I, Mr Masters," he continued. "You're doing astoundingly well. He's probably the most famous person in Britain right now. But do you have an exit strategy?"

"A what?" blinked Maz.

"Well, all this celebrity ballyhoo doesn't last for ever."

Maz looked irritated by the inferences. "Look, what is all this? I'm happy to sit here giving your over-priced 'Chateau Plonk' a good old hammering, and ogle your home-helps, but let's cut to the chase. What is it you're after exactly?"

Taplow stroked his earlobe. "You see we think he could go all the way."

"Oh no! No, no! He's not on the transfer list. He's not for sale," Maz said firmly, then looked over at Johnnie Collins, who had barely spoken. "And where does 'Mad Frankie' fit into all this? Does he snip off my fingers one by one with a pair of bolt-cutters if I don't sign on the dotted?"

"No, no. Nothing so crass," Keith said soothingly. "It's just there might be a way we can help you. Help one another. An end game. An end game way, way beyond *Hello* magazine and inane Saturday night chat shows."

Sir George Henderson, having kept his counsel throughout this discourse, enigmatically sniffed his goblet of wine and broke his silence. "He's a very clever boy…"

"We think he has unimaginable potential," enthused Taplow.

Maz looked increasingly uncomfortable. "Well, I think you should call Lulu-Belle and Sugar-Tits to fetch my coat and call me an Uber. We're done here, gentlemen."

"Oh, dear," Sir George interjected. "We appear to have got off on the wrong foot, Mr Masters."

"You see, we get it," Keith insisted. "You are very obviously the real power behind the throne. The brains. We have no desire to split you up. Far from it, in fact."

Maz settled back into his chair, flattered for the moment, and took a gulp of wine, wondering where this was all leading.

Sir George took over. "This isn't a take-over bid. It's not even a business proposition. Well, not in the traditional sense, at least. We're talking about something much more seductive than even money, Mr Masters. Power."

Johnnie suddenly chipped in, "Which pays well anyway, so it's a win-win."

Maz couldn't resist. "Oh, he is allowed to speak then? Alright. You've got my attention. What sort of power?"

Sir George took a mouthful of wine, then paused for effect. "Since the dawn of time those in power have kept the masses in check by the judicious and liberal use of fear and paranoia. For centuries religions ruled supreme, using fear and paranoia of evil spirits and the devil himself. As religious doctrine became less persuasive than consumerism and greed, our esteemed leaders have kept the great unwashed in their place with fear and paranoia of one another; immigrants; asylum seekers; noisy neighbours; muggers; louts; binge drinkers; football hooligans; foreigners; sex offenders; benefits scroungers; terrorists; the idle rich; the idle poor. We can't even say what we think any more for fear of offending somebody who can't wait to be offended. Forget free speech! That flew right out of the window the day the term political correctness was first coined. We're heading back to the Dark Ages."

Keith took over, with the same fervour in his eyes. "The time is ripe for change. People are restless. Dissatisfied. The fear and paranoia now even extends to the leaders themselves. We don't trust them. We don't even like them. We grudgingly elect the least worst through lack of choice."

Sir George got his second wind. "You are to be congratulated, Mr Masters. What you have created is quite unique. Your boy is not just liked, he is worshipped. People love him. People listen to him."

Maz cut through all the pomposity, demanding some clarity. "I don't see what use he is to you. He bends spoons and helps people cut down on fags and pies."

It worked. Taplow inched nearer to the point. "We're not looking for radical ideas or policies. We already have an infrastructure in place. And a strong manifesto. What we have is a political party which is on the verge of exploding. A massive percentage of the voters are already convinced. The rest are just afraid to admit out loud that they agree with our, er, rather robust political agenda."

Sir George clarified yet further. "What you have, Mr Masters, is something the other parties have been searching for since Churchill. A revered leader. A guiding light. Together we could blow the old guard clean out of the water. We'd be unstoppable."

Collins suddenly chipped in again. "And his accent would stop *Guardian* readers bleating about us being closet racists."

Sir George and Keith looked at Johnnie disapprovingly, not really welcoming his somewhat clumsy intervention.

Maz sat for a moment, letting it all sink in. "So you want a puppet?"

Keith shook his head. "Not a puppet. A figurehead."

Maz nodded noncommittally. "What are we talking here? Mayor of London?"

Sir George smiled. "Mayor of London is a bit of a political cul-de-sac. A thankless job for a die-hard misfit. A fellow who's too useful to lose, but too bonkers to be put anywhere where he can do any real damage."

Realising they were making headway, Keith risked indiscretion. "I'm sure you've heard about the junior minister caught having a little fiddle with his pretty young male intern? Says he's definitely not going to resign and his wife's standing by him. So is the PM. Word is he'll be gone by Friday, which means there will be a by-election."

Sir George then took the bull by the horns and concluded their unholy offer. "If your boy won that by-election for us, which we think he would, then it would be churlish of us not to have a leadership contest, which, strictly entre-nous, we could guarantee he'd win. What do you say, Mr Masters?"

There really was only one thing Maz could say: "Fuck me sideways!"

CHAPTER SIXTEEN

Lindsey and Clive were once again in Wonderland, large glasses of red wine on the table in front of them. Their mood was as dark as the Malbec. BBC Executive Rachel Rashford had secured them a five-minute spot on a live lunchtime current affairs magazine programme, which should have been a cause for celebration. The next day, however, they were licking their wounds from the reaction to their second television appearance together, which had been, at best, lukewarm.

Lindsey took a glug of wine then admitted that the response to their appearance on the programme had been disappointing.

"Disappointing?" snorted Clive. "Downright bewildering! I proved I can do the things he can do."

Lindsey nodded, "I must admit I thought that was far more damning than people seem to think."

Clive couldn't hide his bitterness regarding Serghei. "He could fall headfirst into a cesspit and crawl out smelling of the lavender bush he tripped over!"

Lindsey tried to mitigate the situation. "He's riding high on an incredible wave of good will at the moment, for sure. We knew this wasn't going to be easy. We just have to keep chipping away."

"Your bloody newspaper was one of the worst!" fumed Clive.

"You know I have no control over that," Lindsey said, defensively.

Clive quoted her editor, with understandable resentment, "Some bitter twisted failed magician trying to make a name for himself... Thanks a bunch!"

"I warned you that Derek is very pro-Serghei."

"Why, for God's sake?" Clive gasped, out of sheer exasperation.

"Because he sells papers, that's why. Look, I'm sure we've planted a seed of doubt in some of the more intelligent people's minds. You're not going to give up are you?"

"God, no!" answered Clive. "If anything I'm more determined than ever to prove that I'm the good guy here, and he's the one taking the population for a bunch of mugs."

"That's the spirit," smiled Lindsey, patting his arm. "You'll be a hero when it comes out that you were right all along. You were good yesterday, very good, despite the hostile questioning."

"You think so?" Clive badly needed her reassurance.

"Of course. Your tricks were just as good as his. Really clever. I can see you being the next David Blaine when we've finished with Serghei. Just don't give up, eh?"

Lindsey had moved up close and was touching his arm again, wanting to make him feel good about himself and calm his ire, but no more. Clive, not exactly a man of the world, misread the signs and leaned in, lips puckered, as though to kiss her.

Lindsey was horrified and instinctively moved back. "Oh shit, I'm sorry, Clive. I'm not... I wasn't..."

Clive was mortified. "Oh God, I'm so sorry. I thought you were... I feel such an idiot..."

"Don't worry," Lindsey said, quickly putting some distance between them. "It's fine. Really. It's just, well, you know..."

There was an uncomfortable pause in their conversation, with neither of them quite knowing what to say next.

Clive eventually smiled. "At least I haven't made things awkward..."

Lindsey did have the good grace to laugh.

* * *

Maz was sitting behind his huge desk in his plush office when a sombre-faced Serghei was ushered in. Maz got up, greeted him with a brief manly hug, and steered him towards the white settee in the informal 'comfy area' of his new spacious working domain.

"Grab a pew. How are you doing, champ? Hey, who was that annoying little shit on telly yesterday, trying to do your shtick?"

Serghei grimaced. "I know him. Knew him. He's a total pain in the ass."

"He's not exactly your biggest fan either. So what occurred with him?"

Serghei shrugged and tried to dismiss the question by saying it was a long story.

"And why doesn't that surprise me?" sighed Maz. "Everything always is with you."

"Do we sue him?" asked Serghei. "Get a restraining order or something?"

"Nah, he's just a pest, not a problem. If we set the hounds on him it just makes him a bigger deal. It looks like he's got us rattled. And puts him on the front pages. I think damage limitation is we just ignore the little twat and he'll probably go away. It's back-fired on him anyway, because everybody is just saying how dare anyone doubt poor sweet Serghei? Funny really. So, more importantly, how are things with you and the good Mrs Iliescu?"

Serghei told him not to ask.

"I am asking. This is a problem."

Serghei shrugged, admitting that nothing much had changed between them, and Simona was still ice-cold.

"Don't forget what a disgruntled iceberg did to the Titanic. You've got to sort this, my old love."

Serghei looked deflated. "I am still sleeping in spare room."

Maz shook his head, with a sardonic smile. "Ironic really. The wise guru who sorts out everybody else's problems has the most screwed up life of anybody I know."

Serghei explained that Simona had told him he couldn't go near her until she sees the divorce papers. Of course Maz panicked and told him that wasn't going to happen as Aurelia had gone home. Serghei suggested that their lawyers could surely contact her in Romania.

"No, best let sleeping dogs lie there, I think," Maz interjected, somewhat alarmed. "Anyway, what is it with you and lawyers this morning? Have they got you on commission? Let me have a word with Simona. See if I can do a Kofi Annan."

Seeing Serghei's puzzled expression, he sarcastically explained, "It's a sweet sickly Indian ice cream. Women love it. You really are going to have to brush up on your current affairs and recent history if you're going into politics."

Serghei looked doubtful. "I still don't know about that. All I ever wanted was to be a well-respected magician."

"I think that ship's well and truly sailed. And, if your devoted following ever do find out you're a bloody magician, you'll be about as well respected as Rolf Harris and Gary Glitter."

"What do I know about politics?" asked Serghei, with good reason.

"What did you know about self-help? Sweet fuck-all, until we got on the internet. Six months later you're the bleedin' grand master. Look, I hate to admit it, but Sir George's merry men are right. This media hysteria isn't going to last for ever. Then what? And annoyingly they're also right that we never did have an end game in mind."

Serghei raised his eyebrows, stating that a beach in the Caribbean had always been his end game.

"You'd be bored out your skull within a fortnight. And shagged half the island. What then? It's irritating that we didn't think of it, but we should make use of the fact that you are currently more famous than Jesus. Even if we had thought of it we couldn't have done much about it. They have all the machinery in place. All you've got to do is step in and wallow in the glory. That you are good at."

Serghei remained unconvinced. "But you say they only have one MP. They are losers."

"That's the first-past-the-post voting system for you. They got millions of votes at the last election. People here are desperate for a change from the shit two same-old, same-old parties who seem to think it's their God-given right to swap power from one to the other every few years. With you, 'Golden Bollocks', at the helm, in place of that pint-swilling, chinless good ol' boy buffoon Rupert What's-'is-face, who knows what might happen? What we got to lose? You lose this by-election, people will still love you and think you're even more of a serious player. God loves a trier, an' all that. If you win you're a party leader with the prospects of Adolf in 1934. Alright – bad analogy – but you get my drift."

* * *

Back in the safety of his bedroom Clive was sitting staring into the camera on his laptop, recording the next update for his YouTube vlog.

"Thank you to those of you who have commented on my Twitter page about my appearance on TV yesterday. If any of you missed it you will be able to see it for at least another week on 'catch-up'. It didn't quite have the major impact I was hoping for, but it's a start. I can't breach the magicians' code and tell you how the tricks were done, but I can assure everyone that I wasn't using any paranormal powers. Just sleight of hand and misdirection, but I managed to imitate everything that Serghei does. There is a very simple reason for that. He doesn't have any paranormal powers either. He is using exactly the same sleight of hand and misdirection, because he is no more than a magician himself. People need to know the truth. Deserve to know the truth, even if they don't want to believe it."

The next morning Lindsey was standing behind her boss's shoulder in his office. They were watching that same vlog update from Clive's YouTube channel. Derek dismissively closed his laptop when it was over.

"I hope you're not helping this vindictive little twerp in my time."

"No," said Lindsey. "You made your views very clear. I'm doing this in my own time."

As Lindsey moved round his desk, preparing to leave the office, her editor stopped her. "Listen, if I'm honest, I probably agree with everything you are trying to say, but I'm not about to help you kill the goose that lays the golden eggs. Everything Serghei says or does sells papers. He breaks wind and it's another headline. Our circulation soars. Why would any of us want that state of affairs to end?"

Lindsey looked exasperated. "I know your views. I'm not even sure why we're having this conversation. I've stopped asking you for permission to write an investigative piece."

"It's just a gentle warning," Derek said firmly. "I don't want to catch you using my time or resources for this bloody irritating crusade of yours with 'Boy Wonder'. And I would ask you to let it drop in your spare time as well, but I have a feeling I'd be wasting my breath. But, be warned Lindsey, I will only let you go so far before I cite conflict of interest."

* * *

To the casual observer, Keith Taplow appeared to be having a quiet drink with an acquaintance in his exclusive gentlemen's club, the Barracuda. Of course people like him never switch off. They can't help themselves. A 'quiet drink' was either an attempt to woo a party donor; the forging of some expedient but unholy alliance; or, in this case, the lobbying of a known far-right Tory MP to jump ship and swap political allegiances. This prominent backbencher had already committed the cardinal sin of briefing against his own boss, the Conservative Prime Minister. 'Briefing against' being a quite grownup sounding parliamentary euphemism for the somewhat juvenile act of gossiping behind a friend or ally's back, stirring up trouble and causing mischief.

Of course MPs are only ever interested in being on the winning side, so Taplow had his work cut out to convince this former cabinet minister that his party was making great headway and would soon be a force to be reckoned with. He was promising the kind of right-wing reforms that Tory extremists could only dream of. Keith cursed as his phone began to vibrate in his jacket pocket, interrupting his momentum. He seemed so close to having his prey on the hook. A quick glance at his phone was needed to assess whether the call was more important than reeling in this prize catch. The name came up, 'Maz Masters'. Damn. Potentially this was extremely important, despite the fact that he had taken an instant dislike to Maz.

"Sorry old boy. Forgive me. Must take this," he said to his Tory associate, getting up and sidling into a quiet corner. "Mr Masters. How are you?"

Maz had equal contempt for Taplow, so his response was through gritted teeth. "Maz," he said, correcting Keith's formality, and trying to keep things civil, "I'm good as."

"What news?" enquired Taplow, cutting right to the chase.

"Well if this dodgy caught-with-his-pants-down junior minister does resign I think you have your candidate for the by-election."

"Ah, now that is good news. This rather calls for a celebration. Oh, and don't worry, he will resign. Tomorrow. Or Friday. We should all get together and drink something expensive."

Maz was still cynical. "The timing of this by-election is a bit convenient. In an area where you already have a lot of grassroots sympathy. I'm street-savvy enough to realise it's, likely as not, no coincidence."

"I can't imagine what you mean," smarmed Taplow. "Although somebody with all our best interests at heart may possibly have helped the photographs get into the right hands."

"Bleedin' hell!" Maz exclaimed. "The way politics works makes running a lap dancing club look like organising a parish church coffee morning."

Keith looked around, to check nobody was listening, then posed a vital question: "I know your boy can't put a foot wrong in the public's eye, but there isn't anything we should know?

No big scandal about to erupt?"

Maz feigned surprise. "I'm shocked you even ask!"

With an unexpectedly cold hard edge to his voice Taplow growled, "Let's dispense with the lairy barrow-boy banter just for a moment, Mr Masters. There is far too much at stake here to piss about. For all of us. Is there anything in the closet which might rock the boat?"

Maz, slightly cowed suddenly, answered, "Of course not."

CHAPTER SEVENTEEN

The high-profile governmental resignation was hot news by mid-afternoon the next day. The poor unfortunate junior minister was swamped by TV crews and press photographers, gathering like vultures outside his house, hoping to get a few chastened words from him and a forlorn look from his long-suffering wife.

The ten o'clock television news devoted most of the programme to the story, on both major terrestrial channels.

With unconcealed glee, Tom Preston, the news anchor on ITV, opened with, "A by-election has been called in North Riding, following the resignation this morning of Conservative's Junior Education Minister, Julian Fitzsimmons."

There were then shots of Fitzsimmons scrambling out of a taxi, shielding his face from rapidly flashing cameras and fighting through the media throng, in a dash to his front door.

"Mr Fitzsimmons has made a statement saying he wants to spend more time with his family, and feels his post in cabinet committee is no longer tenable, following sordid and regrettable revelations about his private life. Having foregone this important job, and blown any chance of future promotion, he says he has no desire to continue from the back benches, so he is stepping aside completely, which means his constituency seat is suddenly up for grabs. North Riding has traditionally been a Tory stronghold, but in the last election the British Independence Party gave the Conservatives a run for their money and came a close second, losing out by less than two thousand votes."

There followed shots of Serghei shaking hands with suited figures and waving to the cameras from the doors of the party headquarters.

"In a surprise move, just a few hours ago, the BIP have announced that their candidate in the forthcoming by-election will be the celebrity mystic and self-help guru, Serghei. Our political editor Laura Alexander joins me now. Laura – what are they up to?"

These were the rare kind of days that political reporters positively salivate over, so Laura couldn't contain her delight as she sat in the studio, across the desk from Tom, ready and prepared to pontificate. "Well, politically speaking, they are doing a shrewd bit of re-positioning of the party. The reality of the situation is it's a very clever bit of marketing. Serghei is a hugely popular figure, and has the ear of the ordinary man or woman in the street."

Preston butted in, "With absolutely no parliamentary experience."

"That's very true," agreed Laura, "but not being a politician could play in his favour. Never have conventional career politicians been less popular. Of course the Tories have dismissed his candidacy as a gimmick, a poor joke, and an insult to the electorate and democracy itself, but insiders tell me there is genuine concern within the party that they could lose this previously 'safe seat', which would be a serious blow to the government."

"So what does this mean for the future of the BIP?" asked Tom.

"Well, interestingly, they are going in for some serious re-branding in the run-up to this by-election, probably seeing this as make-or-break time for them as a credible threat to the two-party system. They have just announced, presumably out of deference to their new candidate, that they are changing the name of the party to the Spirit of the Nation. It's a smart and timely reinvention, and a major step towards softening some of the hard edges of the party which undoubtedly frightened off some voters at the last general election."

"Do we know yet what issues they plan to campaign on?"

Laura leaned back, taking a breath and glancing at her notes.

"It's too soon for them to make any formal announcements about their campaign, but they have already said that they will continue to fight for traditional British values and a stronger united country."

Tom smiled irreverently. "Where have we heard that one before? I suppose the sixty-four-thousand-dollar question is: can the Spirit of the Nation win this quite crucial by-election?"

"Absolutely they can," Laura answered confidently. "Serghei's massive popularity with the British public makes him a very strong candidate, arguably a front-runner. And another seat in Parliament would be a massive boost to a party which is gaining popularity all the time. Watch this space!"

"Laura – thank you very much indeed," Tom said, turning back to his main camera. "The Conservative Party have just announced that their new candidate will be thirty-four-year-old Helen Scott, who studied politics and history at Oxford University…"

Newspaper offices were also buzzing with excitement. Derek Hyland had assembled his entire team for their daily brief and, specifically, to discuss their coverage and approach regarding the by-election. They were all watching a recording of the previous night's ITV news on the subject. When it was over he span his chair round to address them all.

"Well, I think it's the most exciting thing to happen in British politics for years. Certainly as far as we are concerned."

Lindsey looked almost sulky at the far end of the long boardroom table. "If it wasn't so scary it would be positively farcical!"

"It's no more ludicrous than that muscle-bound monosyllabic halfwit Schwarzenegger becoming Governor of California," said Hyland, "… or Donald sodding Trump becoming President for that matter."

Lindsey was undeterred. "Doesn't it just go to prove what I've been saying all along? That he's dangerous."

Derek was running out of patience on what should be regarded, in his view, as a good news day. "I'll thank you to keep your personal vendetta out of this Lindsey. There are a lot of column inches in this development, and a lot of papers will be bought in the run-up. No overt political bias, but I don't want anything negative. It's a breath of fresh air at a time when politics has never been more jaded, for Chris'sake."

He then looked around the table, assigning appropriate tasks to his key staff. "Emma – get on to his people and see if we can be first to do a big spread on the real man at the heart of the mythology and media hype. Nice heart-warming human stuff with lots of photos. Phil – you do a more serious piece on his political ambitions and what issues he is campaigning on. And then work with Emma on a follow-up piece: *Is the Tory / Labour stranglehold finally over?* The rest of you – business as usual, but any bright ideas on the by-election coverage will be very welcome. Thank you everybody."

Lindsey lingered as everybody started leaving to get to work. "What about me? Do you want me to put on a fluffy squirrel suit and offer to be his mascot?"

"I've warned you once," Derek said wearily. "I thought you were more professional. You're going nowhere near this. You can take William and Kate at the Chelsea Flower Show…"

* * *

Clive and his mother were sitting side by side in their flat, eating fish and chips from matching floral trays on their laps, watching the teatime news, which included all the latest on the North Riding by-election. Clive stiffened as a shot of Serghei waving to crowds came on screen.

Molly couldn't help herself. "I know you don't like me talking about him, but you have to admit your Russian friend's done well for his-self."

Clive bit his tongue and told his mother, in no uncertain terms, that he didn't want to discuss it.

"It does seem you were wrong about him," she unwisely persisted. "He might be an MP before long."

Clive couldn't take it. "Oh right, yes, because becoming a politician has always been a sign that somebody is honest, trustworthy, and beyond corruption. I sometimes envy you living in your little rose-tinted cocoon."

"It doesn't do any harm looking for the good in people," said Molly. "I'd vote for him."

Clive gasped out of sheer frustration. "You don't even know what he stands for, or what he believes in."

"Well, he can't be any worse than the shower we normally get. And he always looks smartly turned out."

CHAPTER EIGHTEEN

Maz was at his gigantic desk, taking an important call, when he heard a disturbance down the corridor. Raised women's voices were approaching, sounding like two angry geese fighting in a sack. Suddenly his office door burst open and a livid Simona burst in, dragging Kat, Maz's personal assistant, behind her. A flustered Kat was clinging on to Simona's arm, trying to restrain her, but she was no match for the fiery ex-pole-dancer.

"I'm so sorry, Maz," Kat panted breathlessly. "She wouldn't wait. I tried to tell her you were on the phone."

Simona slapped Kat's hands away viciously. "My fucking husban' pays your wages, bitch! Get your skanky hands off of me!"

Maz guessed it wasn't a social visit and Simona wasn't going to sit down quietly while he finished his phone call, so he told the woman on the other end that he'd call her back in ten minutes. Looking again at Simona's raging face he quickly made it twenty minutes, then hung up, reassuring poor Kat that everything was fine, and telling her to leave them. His PA flounced out, readjusting her dishevelled clothes, feeling embarrassed and undermined.

"I'll scratch that fuckin' bitch's eyes out if she touch me again!" Simona shrieked after her.

Maz couldn't resist heavy sarcasm. "And to what do I owe the pleasure of your ever-radiant presence, Mrs Iliescu?"

"I am going to take him for half of everything he owns!"

"Oh that's good," said Maz. "So you're going to leave him one bollock then?"

Simona was not amused. "It is all joke to you! Well see how funny it is when I ruin him! I want half the money. Plus I get apartment and everything in it!"

"So, a bit more than half of everything then, actually?"

Maz realised sarcasm, tempting as it undoubtedly was, was not going to win the day, so he adopted a more soothing tone, trying to guide Simona towards the informal 'comfy area' of his office. "Look, sit down, darling, calm yourself down…"

She wasn't going anywhere. "I don't want sit down! And I don't want to calm down!"

Clearly Serghei's promised attempts at a reconciliation had fallen on deaf ears. In fact it appeared he had poured petrol on the already towering inferno.

Maz somehow manoeuvred Simona to the white settee and physically pushed her down. She reluctantly acquiesced, but sat on the edge of the settee, rather than sitting back and making herself comfortable. Her body language was bordering on the profane. Maz sat next to her and took her hand, patting it, in an attempt to pacify her. "Come on babe, you and me could always talk."

Simona withdrew her hand aggressively. "Don't try to get round me. You always got me to do what you want in the club, but not this time – Babe!"

"I just want what's best for you," Maz said, soothingly. "You know you don't really want to split up with him. He wants you to take him back so bad."

"He make fool of me", snapped Simona. "Did you know he already have a wife? You cover for him."

"Why would I get involved? I know some girls love a bad boy, but I can't imagine busty gangsters' molls flinging 'emselves at me just because I've been had up for aiding and abetting a bigamist. It was as big a shock to me as it was to you."

"He is scumbag. I finish him!"

Maz tried to reassure her that something could be worked out. Anxiously he checked whether she had sought any form of legal advice regarding separation.

Simona just kept ranting, "No way! I don't pay some blood-sucker bastard a hundred quids a minute to write him letter. Not when I know I have him over barrel. He'll pay!"

"So you haven't discussed this with anybody?" asked Maz, breathing a metaphorical sigh of relief. "Other than shrieking at me?"

"No, because I know you will make him settle. I can finish him! And you! I sell my story. I know everything. He is illegal immigrant with forged passport. He is married to two women. He is lying cheating bastard!"

"Well nobody's perfect..." muttered Maz, more to himself than anybody.

But Simona wasn't finished. "And don't forget I know his voodoo so-called mystical powers are just a load of magic tricks. Just see how quick the public learn to hate him as much as me when they find he's been lying to them too!"

Maz bristled at this dire threat and instinctively turned menacing. "If you so much as breathe a fucking word..." He stopped himself, knowing a different, more measured approach was needed, before things got out of hand. "Look, we all agreed, made an oath on our lives. You promised that was something none of us would ever talk about."

"Yes, and he promise he love, honour and fucking cherish!"

* * *

Later that day Maz and Serghei were travelling together in the back of a large, luxury, chauffeur-driven executive car.

Serghei started saying that it looked as though they had no choice and they would have to give Simona half of everything. Maz was alarmed, in case the driver could hear them, even though there was an allegedly sound-proof clear screen, separating the front from the back of the car. He started making taunts about the chauffeur driving like his Nan, and smelling a bit like her as well. When the man kept looking straight out at the road ahead, without even flinching, Maz became satisfied that he wasn't able to hear them, and responded to Serghei's suggestion of surrender.

"And then what happens when she's spent it all? She just comes back again with more threats and the begging-bowl, asking for more. I said you should never have confided in her."

Serghei shrugged, "How was I to know she would blackmail me? Us."

"What a fucking mess," groaned Maz. "I take it you don't want her back now?"

"Would you?"

"You have a point there, my friend," Maz nodded, resignedly. "You'd be just waiting for the day when you walked into the kitchen to find your pet bunny gently bubbling away in the slow-cooker."

Serghei summed up their predicament, "She is crazy person."

"Okay, leave it with me," sighed Maz. "I'll think of something. In the meantime, don't for chris'sake let creepy Keith and the Spirit of the Nazis hear you talking about all this."

"Oh, by the way," said Serghei, now reminded about his newfound political calling. "This chat show they've got me doing to promote the election. I want to do one of my stunts. Paranormal experiments. I don't want people forgetting what I do."

"Yeh, whatever. I'll have a word with the producers."

Right at that moment Maz had much bigger things to worry about than yet another magic trick on a chat show, but he mentally added it to the bottom of his daunting 'to do' list.

The executive car glided to a halt outside the Park Lane hotel where Serghei was staying, since becoming persona totally non grata at home.

* * *

Early evening, Maz was incognito in a large upmarket West End hotel, heading into the end WC cubicle in the Gents cloakroom, adjacent to their Michelin-starred celebrity-chef restaurant. He slid the bolt on the door, having checked there was nobody else around. Carefully he lifted the heavy porcelain lid from the cistern and rested it on the closed lavatory seat. Next he removed the thick tightly-wrapped waterproof package from his coat pocket and tucked it behind the flush mechanism, under the water, before drying his hands on a pocket handkerchief and replacing the cistern lid. Maz flushed the toilet, in case anybody had walked into the cloakroom, and emerged to wash his hands and comb his hair.

Sitting in a quiet corner of the cocktail lounge, downing his second large brandy, he phoned Simona and made an arrangement to buy her dinner at Langan's Brasserie at nine o'clock. It wasn't obvious to anybody around the hotel, where he was a complete unknown, but Maz had the look of a deeply troubled man.

Allowing sufficient time to elapse for Maz to leave the hotel, and dozens of other people to come and go on the CCTV cameras in the restaurant corridor, making any connection between him and Maz impossible to spot, an anonymous looking middle-aged man made his way into the same cloakroom and the same WC cubicle. As stealthily as the waterproof package had been put into the cistern this man removed it, dried it and slipped it into his own coat pocket.

By mid-evening that same shadowy figure was parked within view of the security gates outside Serghei and Simona's luxury apartment block. With the window of his elegant silver Mercedes down he was chain-smoking to pass the time.

At twenty past eight, as expected, a sleek black car from a well-known executive taxi service pulled up at the gate. The man parked nearby tossed his current cigarette into the gutter, got out of his Mercedes, and crossed the road. The driver of the executive taxi also got out of his car, but, before he could press the communication button on the gate, he was intercepted by the shadowy figure.

"You here to pick up Mrs Iliescu? Flat One for Langan's?"

"She didn't say where she was going, but yeh, Flat One. Why? Wassup?" asked the driver.

"She isn't going anywhere now. Changed her mind. She does this. Sorry mate. She sent me out with this." The middle-aged man pressed two twenty-pound notes from his black-gloved hand into the driver's hand.

The executive taxi driver sighed, then looked at the notes, folded them, pocketed them, shrugged, got back into his car and drove off.

A minute or two later the anonymous darkly-clad man got back in his parked Mercedes and moved it across the road, and re-parked it right outside the gated apartment complex. He then got out, pressing the top button on the entry system call-box by the gate.

Within a few moments Simona's curt clipped voice crackled through the speaker, "Yes?"

"Car for Mrs Iliescu."

"Give me five minutes," snapped Simona, ungraciously.

The man lit up yet another cigarette and leaned back against his smart silver saloon car, drawing the soothing smoke deeply into his lungs.

By midnight the almost full moon was bright in the clear star-spangled sky. It reflected poetically in the rippling inky black water of the reservoir on the bleak deserted Berkshire moor. The man with the Mercedes was dragging a heavily-weighted and tightly-wrapped human-shaped canvas sack along the walkway on top of the dam. With a supreme effort and a loud involuntary grunt, he breathlessly managed to hump the sack over the low wall when he reached the middle. The splash was loud, making an alarmed owl flap noisily away, but it was unheard by any other human.

The smoke from his freshly-lit cigarette looked almost blue in the eerie moonlight as the man watched the last bubbles rise from the deep icy cold water.

An hour later, nearly forty miles away, in a back-street of Reading, there was the low crump of a petrol tank exploding, accompanied by a soaring orange plume. A stolen Mercedes was being torched.

CHAPTER NINETEEN

It was the first time Lindsey had ventured back into Wonderland with Clive for quite some time. They were self-consciously sitting a little distance apart as they sipped their usual large glasses of Malbec.

"I haven't heard from you in a while," Clive began. "I thought maybe I'd... I'm so sorry about last time. I just thought..."

"It's okay. Really," Lindsey said with a reassuring smile. "But let's just keep things professional. I'm sure you're just as horrified as I am by the latest twist in the Serghei saga."

"Totally," Clive nodded. "He's got to be stopped."

"Through a friend of a friend I've heard he's going on Charlotte Allen's late-night chat show this week to talk about the election, but apparently he's going to do a couple of his paranormal ESP experiments, or whatever he calls them."

Clive couldn't resist correcting her, "Magic tricks."

"Well that's the thing," Lindsey said, sitting forward and getting animated. "Apparently Charlie has always been a bit sceptical. Her grandfather was a magician, I think. So they can get you backstage to take a look at his props."

Clive shook his head. "He'll never leave them lying around, out of his sight. He's way too cunning for that."

"Alright," continued Lindsey, thinking on her feet. "So maybe you plant something of your own. I don't know. There must be something you can do to trip him up. It's live you see, so he can't wriggle out of it if anything goes wrong for him, or something gets exposed as a trick."

At that moment Lindsey Montgomery's heart sank. She could see her reporter colleagues Emma and Phil walking in through the door, and they had spotted her.

"Oh shit!" exclaimed Lindsey, as her workmates waved and started walking towards them.

Much to Clive's surprise she quickly sidled up close to him and urgently started talking to him out of the corner of her mouth, like a third-rate ventriloquist. "Sorry Clive, I haven't got time to explain, but you're going to find this really confusing. I apologise in advance, but it's unavoidable. Just go with it, please."

Lindsey cosied up to Clive and quickly took his hand in hers as Emma and Phil approached, all smiles.

"Hiya," said Lindsey warmly. "I didn't know you two came here. This is my boyfriend, Clive. Clive – this is Emma and Phil, colleagues from the paper."

Clive didn't have a clue what was going on, but quite liked the premise behind the duplicity, so, obligingly, played ball. "Oh right, yes. Hi. Nice to meet you both."

Emma, unfortunately, seemed to recognise him. "We've met before, haven't we?"

Lindsey intercepted the question, trying to deflect it. "I don't think so. We haven't been dating long."

"You look so familiar," Emma persisted. "I'm sure I know you."

Phil snapped his fingers, having solved the conundrum for his workmate. "You're the magic guy! Serghei's nemesis."

Lindsey rather overdid the acting. "Oh yes, of course – that'll be how you recognise him. That's how we met, and, you know, one thing led to another."

Emma turned to Clive, who was thinking 'if only': "So what do you think about him becoming a politician and standing for Parliament?"

Lindsey tried to stop the conversation by insisting they shouldn't be talking 'shop' at this time in the evening, but Phil encouraged Clive to have his say, as it was an interesting question.

"Well," said Clive, "I think he'll fit in very well to be honest. He's already got all the necessary attributes. Deceitful, insincere, and always swerves the difficult questions."

They all laughed, but Lindsey looked decidedly uncomfortable.

It seemed like a lifetime, but eventually Phil and Emma made a polite withdrawal, to leave 'the two lovebirds' in peace. Lindsey dropped Clive's hand like it had magically turned into a scalding hot potato, and shuffled away, apologising profusely and trying to explain that, as far as her boss was concerned, she had given up her crusade against Serghei, so she'd had to come up with a plausible excuse for being seen with 'Boy Wonder', as Derek insisted on calling him.

Clive had enjoyed the warm softness of her hand, the touch of her thigh against his, and the all-too-brief subterfuge, so he felt the apology was a little too vehement for his liking. Nevertheless, they ordered another drink and started formulating a plan to derail Serghei's appearance on Charlotte Allen's chat show.

* * *

It was Friday night, around ten past eleven, live on ITV. The studio floor manager was cueing enthusiastic applause from the audience as they returned on-air after the second commercial break. A young female singer and a heart-throb actor were already sitting on the long sofa, as Charlie Allen smiled her award-winning smile from behind her desk, and took her cue, through her earpiece, from the director's box:

"My final guest this evening is nothing short of a phenomenon. Eighteen months ago nobody had ever heard of him. Since then, thanks to his extraordinary psychic abilities, he's become just about the most famous man in Britain. Now the self-help guru wants to help his country and has thrown his hat into the world of politics. We'll of course be talking all about that, but he's also promised to amaze us with some of his gobsmacking paranormal experiments. Will you please put your hands together for – Serghei!!"

The crowd erupted and Serghei walked out to tumultuous applause, bowing and putting his hands together towards the audience, as if in prayer, before approaching the sofa. He warmly shook the hands of the other guests, then turned to acknowledge the host, who had come out from behind her desk for a brief welcoming showbiz kiss.

As she returned to her chair and Serghei made himself comfortable on the sofa, near her desk, a props man entered with a large tray, which he placed on the long low table in front of the guests. The tray was covered with an assortment of spoons, forks, keys, nails, cyclists' drink bottles, wristwatches and a sealed A4 manilla envelope. Serghei looked puzzled. His eyes narrowed.

"Thanks so much for finding the time to come on the show this evening, Serghei," Charlie said warmly.

He eyed the tray with suspicion and irritation. "This worries me. What is this?"

Charlie waved her hand towards the tray of props. "Well we just put a few things together. You tell us what you would like to try. What you'd like to demonstrate tonight. You choose. Only do what you want to do."

Serghei looked extremely uncomfortable and decidedly rattled. "I'll maybe try when I feel up to doing something, okay?"

Ms Allen smiled, beginning to wonder if she already had him on the ropes. "That's what I mean. I understand. I have heard you say before that you need to be in the right mindset. And sometimes you have to pass on a particular thing because the moment isn't right. Is that true?"

"That's true," said Serghei, shuffling in his seat. "I really have to be in the zone, the right zone, to do things and make them happen. And many times nothing significant happens. And it doesn't matter if I'm in front of ten people or ten million people, I can only do my best. What I'm saying is I need to have the time to make things happen. If I had time to focus on some of these things, two hours, two days, you know, then of course something would happen…"

Charlie wasn't letting him off the hook. "Well we are live, as you know, and these lovely people have homes to go to, so we don't have unlimited time, but I'm sure there's something here…"

Serghei was getting annoyed. "You know it's not just about *my* mindset. It is also about the people watching wanting me to succeed. I sense a lot of negativity and hostility here."

"I'm sorry you feel that way. I promise you I want to see these things happen as much as anybody does. What about the envelope? One of the members of our team did some drawings and double-sealed them in there. I understand you can tell us what those drawings are, without touching the envelope, just by the power of your mind, X-ray vision, or whatever. Would you like to try that first?"

Serghei gasped, desperately trying to contain his irritation, and maintain some sort of credibility. "Maybe later, when I am psyched sufficiently. It seems to me you are deliberately putting me under a lot of pressure."

Charlie smiled encouragingly. "I really don't mean to. You set the pace. There are a variety of things on the table that you have used in demonstrations before. What would you like to do first?"

Serghei tried a different tack. "Why don't you ask me some more questions?"

Charlie grinned mischievously. "Okay – What's the capital of Bolivia?"

The audience laughed at her joke, but Serghei wasn't in the slightest bit amused.

"I'm sorry. I'm not trying to put you down here," the host apologised, before twisting the knife again. "We put water in just one of those ten cyclists' drink bottles. I've seen you do this. It's very clever. You pass your hand over the top, without touching the bottles, and find the one with the water."

Serghei was beginning to flounder. "You have to understand these are not controlled conditions. You know I find it very strange that one of your production team came into my dressing room and read me fifteen or twenty questions that she said you were going to ask me, about the upcoming election."

Charlie did another disarming smile. "Absolutely. I can ask questions all night, but your people actually said that you particularly wanted to do some demonstrations of your powers tonight." Charlie then turned her back on her disarmed guest and looked at the camera. "We have to take a break now – we'll be right back…"

Maz was absolutely livid. Like an enraged bull he thundered into the director's gallery. "What the fuck is this?"

"I'm sorry, Mr Masters. You can't come in here!" exclaimed the director's PA, getting up and trying to force him back with a withering glare.

It was going to take more than that.

"This is a fucking ambush!" he yelled.

Fortunately for the director's team Maz's phone started to ring.

That gave the PA all the authority she needed. "No mobile phones in the gallery during a live broadcast! Somebody call security."

Maz held up his hands in surrender, one of them containing the offending ringing phone. He backed out of the door he had just come through, glancing down at the name of the caller on his mobile and groaning to himself.

He cursed loudly, then swiped the screen to take the call. "Maz Masters!"

Keith Taplow's voice was cold, yet menacingly calm. "I'm not enjoying my late-night television viewing, Mr Masters. Do something!"

Maz sighed deeply before slumping back against the corridor wall and closing his eyes.

Back in the studio the floor manager was already counting out of the short commercial break and cueing Charlotte Allen once again.

Charlie smiled into her camera. "During the break Serghei was telling me he doesn't feel strong tonight."

Serghei corrected her, irritably, "My *powers* are not strong tonight. I was invited here to talk about the North Riding by-election and me being the Spirit of the Nation candidate. That is where my focus is at the moment. I need focus for my demonstrations. My experiments."

Charlie was insistent. "Of course we want to talk about that, but your people did specifically say that you wanted to perform some..."

Serghei didn't let her finish. "You are giving me a hard time here. I suspect you have a political agenda of your own. Which way do you vote, Ms Allen?"

For the first time it was Charlie who was wrong-footed. "Well, I don't really want to... Well certainly not for the BIP or the Spirit of the Nation, or whatever you are called this week, that's for sure."

Serghei suddenly was able to look righteously indignant. "That is what this is really all about, isn't it? I thought you TV people were supposed to show no political bias."

Serghei stood up, unclipping his personal microphone, and addressing the audience, "I apologise to you, my friends, who genuinely came to listen, but you can see that I am not being allowed to speak freely here, so I am afraid this woman has left me no choice. With regret I must terminate this interview."

The audience applauded wildly. Serghei shrugged with feigned disappointment, threw his microphone down onto the sofa, and walked off, not looking at the host, but waving towards the audience, earning him huge cheers.

The director had risen animatedly to his feet in the gallery. There was a frisson of real excitement.

"Say something Charlie!" he shouted towards the microphone on his desk. "Any fucking thing! Then put the band on – give us time to think!"

The director turned to his team. "This is fucking great television! They'll still be showing this clip as a classic chat show moment in twenty years' time! Good job everybody! Camera Five stay on him! He's still in the wings!"

* * *

Sir George Henderson left it until after he'd had time to peruse the Saturday morning headlines, before he pronounced his verdict on the Charlotte Allen chat show debacle. In the Barracuda Club, just as soon as the sun was over the yard-arm, he and Keith Taplow clinked glasses of single malt Highlands Scotch and ice.

Sir George took a sip. "I thought your boy did really rather well last night."

"In the end," Taplow said, with a somewhat jaded smile. "At first I began to think we'd made a serious error of judgment."

Sir George raised an eyebrow, unhappy that there remained any doubt. "As the song says, it's not where you start it's where you finish."

"He did turn it round remarkably well, I have to say," agreed Keith.

"He's a clever boy."

It was Keith's turn to raise an eyebrow. "I'm not sure 'clever' would be my word of choice. 'Cunning' perhaps. Like a cornered fox."

"Cunning is good," mused Henderson. "Foxes are survivors."

"I seriously thought the game was up," Taplow admitted ruefully.

Sir George couldn't resist a self-satisfied smirk. "The papers are all roasting that blasted Allen woman this morning. How could she be so beastly to our poor beloved Serghei?"

Keith snorted with wry amusement. "Ironically it's ended up a PR triumph."

Henderson gazed into his glass, rolling the ice cubes around with a pleasing clinking sound, then looked up, with a grave expression. "No more scares like that though, eh? We are on the cusp here. We may never have another opportunity like this. Throw everything at him. No expense spared. He must win that seat."

"I have what you might call the ultimate clincher," Taplow said darkly.

"Probably better I don't know," murmured Sir George, downing his Scotch. "Probably better I don't know..."

* * *

That same lunchtime, Clive and Lindsey were sitting on a bench by the lush, verdant bank of the Serpentine in Hyde Park, eating sandwiches and tossing odd crumbs onto the sun-dappled water to feed the swans.

"I really thought we'd totally exposed him last night as a fraud," Lindsey muttered, dejectedly.

"We did!" Clive fumed. "The trouble is it doesn't seem to have made the slightest bit of difference."

"The real problem is nobody wants to know the truth," Lindsey sighed. "As my old grandmother used to say, there are none so deaf as those who don't want to hear."

Clive shook his head. "It's like he has this charmed existence."

Lindsey nodded. "Derek, my editor, calls it the Teflon syndrome."

There was a moment or two of silence, as they enjoyed the tranquil view, then Lindsey looked up. "We should maybe throw ourselves into supporting the Conservative candidate, much as it goes against the grain."

Clive looked doubtful. "I'm not interested in the politics side of it all."

"He could seriously win this by-election," Lindsey warned. "Do you seriously want him to become an MP?"

"All I want to do, all I ever wanted to do, was to expose him as a magician. I can't stand the smug cynical deceit. Pretending to be something he's not."

Lindsey needed to convince her co-conspirator. "It's all

becoming inextricably linked. You and I may be coming at this from different directions, but we want the same thing in the end."

Clive still wasn't convinced. "But you're saying he's untouchable."

"Nobody's untouchable," Lindsey said, almost to convince herself as much as to convince Clive.

CHAPTER TWENTY

Keith Taplow and Johnnie Collins were travelling together to the party headquarters. There was much to be done. They were sitting in the back of Keith's chauffeur-driven Bentley, enjoying the calm comfort and luxury before the hectic work of the day began. As usual everything they said to one another was laced with a dark menace.

Taplow's chauffeur was long-serving, trusted and had heard it all, so there was no need for Keith to be guarded. "Helen Scott is holding a public meeting on Saturday to set her stall out against our boy. It would be a PR disaster for the Tories if things turned ugly."

"How ugly?" asked Collins.

"She's one of these woke snowflakes who bang on about journalists trying to make female politicians conform to expected standards of appearance. Let's see how true to her principles she really is. My guess is it would still rattle her cage if she got something unpleasant on her nice new frock."

"Eggs or paint?" Collins enquired with an alarmingly cool callousness.

Keith shook his head. "Paint is a bridge too far. Gets sympathy from the *Daily Mail* readers. The great unwashed just laugh and ridicule them when they get pelted with half a dozen free-range. A coach-load of knuckle-draggers as well, I think. Oh, and I've a rather special job for your associate, Duggan."

Johnnie took a sharp intake of breath. "He's an arm and a leg."

"Is he still the best?"

"Top of the premier division."

"Then he's worth every penny. A mistake would be unthinkable."

*   *   *

Maz and Serghei were walking across the gated compound outside Simona and Serghei's apartment, towards the outer lobby door. They were both uncharacteristically silent. Maz was wrapped up in his own thoughts and Serghei looked unusually anxious.

Maz unlocked and pushed open the apartment door, handing Serghei the key and revealing the deep-cleaned place to be forensically spotless and tidy.

"You sure she isn't here?" Serghei enquired, looking around nervously. It was as though he was half expecting a crazed Simona to break through the closed bedroom door, at any moment, with a felling axe, screaming, *"Here's Johnny!"*

Maz pushed open all the doors to reassure him. "The place is completely empty. Yours again. It's like she never existed."

"Where did she go?"

"Back to Prague, I suppose," shrugged Maz, brushing the matter aside. "I didn't ask. What's it matter? She's gone."

Serghei looked puzzled. "Strange she didn't phone."

"What? You wanted a farewell ear-bashing, did you?" asked Maz incredulously. "What the fuck's the matter with you?"

"You say she will come back when the money is all gone."

Maz shook his head. "I dug deep enough that's not going to happen."

"How fucking deep? How much you give her?" demanded Serghei.

Maz looked miffed. "I presume that's Romanian for thank you..."

There were a few moments' silence while Serghei wandered around, re-assimilating himself with the place, puzzled at the pristine nature of everything. It was like a show home. Eventually he sat down on the white leather corner sofa, let out a huge sigh, and plunged his head into his hands. In a rare human moment, which few people ever saw, he looked up at his business partner, friend and mentor and asked, "What the hell are we doing, Maz?"

Maz was so wrong-footed by this atypical glimpse of vulnerability he dropped his usual lairy front, chuckled and admitted, "God only knows, my friend. Same as every other chancer on the planet. In search of that elusive pot of gold. Every time we see a rainbow we run towards it like bleedin' headless chickens, and dig."

Serghei looked around, not at the apartment, but at the whole world. "This. All this. It wasn't what we have in mind."

Maz smiled. "To be fair we didn't have a Scooby's what we had in mind."

"But freakin' politics?" Serghei said, raising his arms in the air in despair.

"Look," said Maz sagely, "when life gives you lemons, stop playing the trumpet and start drinking gin and tonic. In any case I've seen it in your eyes – you're loving a glimpse of power."

* * *

Lindsey and her flatmate Shanice were both in the functional kitchen area of their basic but clean two-bedroomed flat in North Acton. Lindsey was opening a tin of food for her black and white cat, 'Bojangles', and Shanice was busy cooking. A small television set was on in the corner. Lindsey put the bowl on the floor for a grateful Bojangles, then asked Shanice how her day had been.

Her flatmate smiled. "Pretty good, as it goes. Saw Lance again. Cosy lunch."

"You shagged him yet?" enquired Lindsey.

"We haven't actually snogged, as such," Shanice grinned, shaking her head. "He did manage a peck on the cheek goodbye."

"Gay!"

"Don't think so. Just needs a rocket up his ass."

"So long as that's all he wants up there. Something smells good," Lindsey said, changing the subject.

"What? Bojangles' cat food?"

"No. The spag bol…"

"Chicken risotto," Shanice corrected her, holding up a fancy bottle. "With truffle oil."

"Yeh, that! Is there any left in that box of rosé?"

"Think so. It's in the fridge. You out later? I'm just going to veg out in front of *Love Island*."

Lindsey heard the title music for the Saturday teatime news, and reached for the TV remote control, quickly turning up the volume. "Sorry Shan – just want to catch the headlines."

The weekend news anchor started gravely, "A police officer is in a critical condition in hospital this evening after violence broke out at a by-election campaign rally for the Conservative party in North Riding earlier today."

Shanice was concentrating on her risotto, so Lindsey called over, "Shit – have you seen this?"

The bulletin continued, "A spokesperson for the hospital confirmed that a male officer in his early thirties was admitted earlier today with serious head injuries. In a statement they said his condition, whilst serious, has been stabilised, but it is too early to tell whether there has been any permanent brain damage. The start of the rally was delayed when Conservative candidate Helen Scott was struck by two eggs as she walked towards the podium, and she had to back-track to clean herself up."

There were gratuitous close-ups of the poor woman reacting to the eggs hitting her, and her personal bodyguard dragging her to safety, whilst his colleague violently grabbed a thug in the audience.

"During this enforced hiatus in the proceedings, violence broke out between security guards and rowdy elements in the gathered crowd. The violence escalated when police officers, armed with riot shields and batons, stepped in to restore order."

More gratuitous shots followed of the savage mayhem between uniformed police and thugs.

Lindsey looked shocked. "I recognise one of those meat-heads. He was at that anti-austerity march a few months ago. I'm sure it's him."

The female news anchor looked grim. "Helen Scott's campaign has undoubtedly been marred by these ugly scenes. We go live now to North Riding where our political editor June Ellis is at the scene…"

June Ellis, clearly revelling in the glory of being the journo on the spot, began a blow-by-blow account, repeating most of what the anchor in the news studio had just said, illustrated by more unnecessarily upsetting shots of the violent clashes, plus an indefensible slow-motion action replay of the egg-throwing.

"Dear God!" gasped Lindsey, both at the events, and at the sensational nature of the insensitive coverage.

The same news bulletin was on the television set in front of Clive and his mother, as they ate their pizzas from the floral trays on their laps, but they were oblivious to the unpleasant story unfolding. They were too busy bickering, as usual.

"Please don't tell me you went to see another medium?" Clive gasped in exasperation.

"She's good this one. She's been on *This Morning* with Phillip Schofield, and she's got a book out. Celebrities go to her. Coleen Nolan, she does."

"Oh, Mum!" Clive sighed. "How many more times do I have to tell you? They are all frauds."

"Doris Stokes wasn't," Molly snapped back.

"Of course she was!"

"You're not old enough to remember."

"I remember she was exposed as a fraud. She used to plant people in the audience. Stooges."

"You always have to know better, don't you?" his mother said, as though Doris Stokes' downfall was somehow his fault.

At that precise moment a shot of Serghei came on the news bulletin. He was doing a walkabout in the busy shopping precinct of a major town in North Riding, shaking hands with awestruck passers-by and waving at passing traffic.

"Don't say a word!" snarled Clive at his mother.

Molly had just been about to comment on Serghei's nice suit, but she wisely bit her tongue.

* * *

With still over two weeks to go before the by-election, bookies were only offering even odds on a Serghei win, as, according to opinion polls, he was merely a couple of percentage points behind the Conservative's Helen Scott. The political pundits were having a field-day and feathers were becoming decidedly ruffled within Westminster. Even the heavyweight political analysts were beginning to acknowledge that, like it or not, celebrity mania and politics are becoming inextricably linked, citing the case of Boris Johnson having risen to prominence off the back of a couple of endearingly bumbling appearances on *Have I Got News for You*, and his lovable rogue of a father enduring Bushtucker Trials in the Australian jungle with Ant & Dec. Nobody quite dared mention the narcissistic host of America's version of *The Apprentice* alarmingly having once become the volatile leader of the Western world.

Serghei was doing the rounds for photo opportunities – kissing babies, cynically being photographed with sick children in hospital, comically extruding phallic pork sausages in the local butcher's shop, and wearing a hard hat and a high-vis jacket to drive a forklift truck through a factory warehouse, for no reason that anybody could fathom.

In desperation, to counter this well-orchestrated and highly successful PR exercise, the beleaguered Tory Prime Minister had left the safety of her ivory tower and was helping Helen Scott with a door-to-door charm offensive around the more affluent areas of North Riding. Unfortunately, she was receiving more abuse than promises of votes.

With ten days still to go the gap had narrowed and the pollsters were saying it was too close to call who was in the lead. The bookies were now refusing to take any more bets on a Serghei win, fearing a devastating financial hit.

Keith Taplow had organised a huge weekend rally for the Spirit of the Nation in North Riding, to try to tip the balance as the by-election drew ever nearer. They had hired a playing field in the centre of the biggest town and had erected an impressively large platform, from which Serghei could address his throng of supporters. Television cameras were going to be there, as was the might of the press. Thanks to Serghei this minor by-election had become a story of national interest and significance.

* * *

On the day of the rally an inconspicuous looking forty-odd-year-old man of average height and average build was walking through the streets of that same large town in the North Riding. He was carrying a black holdall and was dressed predominantly in grey. The man stopped at a door almost invisibly sandwiched between two high street shops and unlocked it with gloved hands, slipping in, unnoticed.

Serghei was inside a large Winnebago, preparing for his big speech. He was surrounded by his support team, which naturally included Maz, plus Keith Taplow, Johnnie Collins, Sir George Henderson, and a couple of young earnest-looking party aides. The walls were adorned with eye-catching posters saying, 'Vote Serghei – the Spirit of the Nation'.

A makeup artist was fussing with Serghei's hair, and asking him if he wanted her to use some hairspray to keep it in place.

Serghei declined at first, thinking only of his macho bravado, but Keith intervened, "I think it might be a good idea Serghei. There's a bit of a breeze today. We don't want any unfortunate photographs."

Serghei shrugged resignedly, so the makeup artist generously lacquered his hair.

"Nervous?" Maz asked.

"Not really," Serghei said, wafting away the choking

hairspray fumes.

Keith chipped in, "You did well with the autocue this morning. It's a stirring speech. Don't forget to pause if they applaud or cheer."

"He does a two-hour stage show," said Maz. "Trust me – he knows how to milk it with an audience."

Sir George looked at Serghei through his reflection in the makeup mirror. "Do you feel the hand of history on your shoulder?"

"Should I?" asked Serghei.

Sir George nodded solemnly. "Today could be the genesis of a seismic shift in the whole political landscape. I'd say you are indeed about to make history, dear boy."

The man in grey was inside a small, dingy, top-floor studio flat above the high street shops. It smelt fusty and slightly damp, as though it had been unoccupied for several months. He dumped the holdall on to the bed and went to check that the rusty wrought iron fire escape was clear, just in case. He then opened the back window to let the stale air escape, and looked out at his clear uninterrupted view of the playing field and the empty platform, decorated with banners heralding the Spirit of the Nation and, more importantly, Serghei. Another colourful banner simply said, 'Are We Ready For Change?' A surprisingly large crowd had already gathered to watch the imminent rally. Satisfied with his vantage point, the man in grey went to the bed, unzipped the holdall and started unpacking the contents.

Inside the Winnebago, the makeup artist was taking the apron away from around Serghei, allowing him to stand up and brush himself down. He cleared his throat, betraying some growing nerves. Maz came up and gave him a big bear hug, feeling surprisingly emotional all of a sudden. Sir George nodded approvingly to Keith Taplow, then patted Serghei on the back to wish him luck.

Serghei stepped out of the Winnebago, which had been conveniently sited behind the platform, and was greeted by two beefy security guards who, rather unnecessarily, escorted him the few yards to the steep steps up to the stage. Serghei took little notice of the uniformed paramedics who were standing by.

Everybody inside the Winnebago was watching the monitor feed from the main video camera. They couldn't help beaming with satisfaction at the tremendous cheer which rang out as Serghei stepped out onto the platform. If there had been a roof on the playing field the crowd would have lifted it.

As Maz had promised, Serghei was an expert at milking the audience reaction. He strode confidently from one side of the stage to the other, backwards and forwards, waving at his supporters and holding his hands over his head like a prize fighter after a championship victory.

Eventually the cheering began to wane, so he headed for the lectern with the microphone and unobtrusive, clear autocue screen.

Like a rock star he shouted, "Hello good people of North Riding! Are we ready for change?"

The audience cheered back, louder than ever. It seemed they were.

'Are We Ready For Change?' had become Serghei's catchy slogan for the by-election, and was proving even more effective at galvanising undecided voters than the irritating mantra, 'Get Brexit Done'.

Serghei expertly waited for the massive cheer to subside before he carried on, "How nice to see so many of you here today. Thank you all.

I think you are here because you really do want to see change. Is there anybody here who can honestly say they are happy with the way our country is governed? We are sick and tired of worthless committees of chauffeur-driven, over-paid, mealy-mouthed Oxbridge clones and grammar-school clowns pretending they know what it's like to live in the real world. We lurch from left to right, desperate to eradicate the mistakes of the incumbents, knowing deep down we will remain in the middle, on the fence, and nothing will change other than the colour of the Prime Minister's rosette. I think you are here because you don't want to have to look the next generation in the eye and admit we knew that the lunatics were running the asylum, and we had the chance to do something about it, but we just couldn't be bothered. It was too much like hard work…"

In the top-floor studio flat everything was assembled and ready. The man in grey had spread a plastic sheet on the floor around him, to catch any forensic evidence, and was carefully following the words of Serghei's speech from the A4 print-out next to him on the windowsill, awaiting his cue…

The crowd were cheering ever more enthusiastically as Serghei made each point with increasing fervour and conviction. "We have a real opportunity my brothers and sisters. An opportunity to rekindle the Spirit of the Nation, to start over, and, with God's help, for Britain to be truly Great once again…"

At that precise moment a single gunshot exploded noisily, and Serghei crumpled to the floor.

CHAPTER TWENTY-ONE

The gathered crowd were in shock. Some screamed, some were rendered silent in disbelief. The security guards and the paramedics had run on stage and were surrounding Serghei's prostrate, bloody body.

Inside the Winnebago, where they had seen the unbelievable atrocity on the television monitor, it was as though everything had gone into slow motion. Maz had collapsed to his knees, howling like a wounded animal, and clutching his head in his hands. Sir George looked shattered and was shouting at everybody to call for an ambulance, before he caught a glimpse of the concerned yet knowing glance between Keith Taplow and Johnnie Collins.

The young party aides frantically dashed out of the door, unsure what to do, but wanting to help. A few moments later one of them returned. She opened the door, looking white as a sheet, her eyes sparkling with tears. She gasped, "They're saying he's dead!"

Maz threw back his head in horror and grief, hollering indistinguishable curses and obscenities. There was another look between Keith and Johnnie – this time a look of panic. Sir George, for once in his life, had no idea what to do or say.

Duggan was carrying the holdall once again as he inconspicuously let himself out of the door between the two shops and walked briskly off, mingling seamlessly with the passers-by, disappearing into the milling throng of weekend shoppers. There were distant sounds of the approaching sirens of mobilised emergency vehicles. In a trice the man in grey had vanished without trace, leaving nothing for them to find.

* * *

Lindsey was open-mouthed as she stood watching the breaking ITN news bulletin in her shared flat.

"Serghei Iliescu, popular TV mystic and self-help guru, now a candidate for the Spirit of the Nation Party, was shot this afternoon during a political rally for the upcoming by-election in North Riding," the weekend news anchor announced gravely. "A spokesperson for the local hospital confirmed that Mr Iliescu had been admitted with serious gunshot injuries, and said that he was in a critical, but stable condition. An unknown gunman appears to have fired a single shot from a nearby building. June Ellis is at the scene. June – what else do we know about the would-be assassin?"

June Ellis, their political editor, had been there to cover the rally, so was first to report on the shocking news. "Very little really. But it appears to have been a professional job, not least because they seem to think that the gun used was a high-powered military grade rifle, accurate up to a distance of over a third of a mile…"

Lindsey was phoning Clive. "Is your TV set on?" she asked in a hushed voice.

Clive could barely speak. "Yes. I don't know what… I don't think I can…"

"No, look," Lindsey firmly interrupted. "This just proves we were right. There is something big going down here."

"Too big!" stammered Clive. "I'm way out of my league. Over my head. I'm just a jobbing close-up magician. I don't want to get…"

"It's more important than ever that we keep doing what we're doing," insisted Lindsey.

"I'm not sure about that…"

* * *

A distraught Maz was sitting by the hospital bed in an expensive private room off the Intensive Care Unit. Serghei was lying motionless on his back, eyes closed, with tubes and pipes going into or coming out of every orifice. Liquids hung in bags from stands, propelled at intervals into Serghei's veins. Monitors with brightly coloured scrolling graphic read-outs pinged and peeped periodically. Other than that the only sound was Serghei's laboured, but unassisted breathing.

The door opened. Maz turned round, expecting to see a nurse or a doctor with news. He was disappointed. It was Keith Taplow.

"How is he?" Taplow enquired quietly.

Maz got up to eyeball the unwelcome visitor. "Skipping up and down, whistling popular hits of the day! How do you think he is? He's been fucking shot!"

Keith was equally hostile. "Frankly, I can live without your sarky banter right now, Masters. I mean he's stable? Right?"

"He's lost a lot of blood and his leg's shot to fuck, but he's not within kicking distance of a bucket if that's what you mean. But neither is he likely to get a call from *Strictly* any time soon."

Keith seemed cold-hearted and rather callous. "We need to issue some sort of press statement."

"We?" yelled Maz, losing his cool.

"About the by-election. Just to let his supporters know he's still around to fight another day."

"You are un-fucking-believable!" snarled Maz. "I don't give a stuff about the sodding by-election! He's having no more to do with that shit!"

Keith frowned. "That's not really your decision to make, Mr Masters."

Maz raised his voice again, "Well it's certainly not yours!"

Hearing this heated exchange, a senior nurse dashed in, looking concerned and annoyed. She hissed angrily at the two overgrown schoolboys. "This is a hospital ward, not a saloon bar in the Wild West! Take your petty squabbles outside! Mr Iliescu is in a very fragile state."

Keith tried to soothe her. "I'm very sorry. We're just having trouble dealing with this. It's been a terrible shock. We were hoping to talk to him."

The nurse relaxed a little. "He's heavily sedated. Are you family?"

Maz butted in, "I'm his bezzy mate. It won't happen again, darling."

The nurse immediately prickled and became angry again. "And you can cut the patronising 'darling' crap as well. I think it's time you both left. He won't be conscious for hours!"

In the middle of the night there was a bit of a commotion. Serghei regained consciousness and he was angry. He tried to sit up and started tugging at the intravenous tubes and pipes, attempting to tear them out. Fortunately, there was a duty night nurse in there, keeping an eye on him at the critical moment. She tried to restrain him and managed to hit the emergency alarm at the same time. Her years of experience showed as she managed single-handedly to calm Serghei down.

A few minutes later there were two doctors in there, one a recently-qualified junior, shadowing her senior counterpart. The nurse was still in there, patting Serghei's hand. He was sitting motionless, angrily staring out into space.

"I can't feel my legs!" Serghei wailed. "I can't feel my fucking legs!"

The senior doctor spoke to him reassuringly, but firmly: "You are heavily anaesthetised. You wouldn't feel a train hitting you right now. You have been shot, Mr Iliescu. The good news is you are going to be fine. The wound is not life-threatening, even though you lost quite a bit of blood. The bad news is the bullet has done some pretty serious damage to your left knee. I think we can save the leg, but there is quite a lot of reconstructive surgery needed."

As soon as Maz woke up the next morning he phoned the hospital from his hotel suite for an update on Serghei's progress. He was relieved to hear that he had regained consciousness, and was even more relieved to hear that he was ill-tempered and giving the staff a hard time. That meant he was already getting back to normal. Maz was still angry, however. He'd been told by the nurse to take his fight with Taplow elsewhere, so that's what he was about to do.

As soon he was showered and shaved he phoned Keith. Dispensing quickly with any pseudo pleasantries, and having communicated a curt version of the hospital update, Maz got to the point and was seriously questioning the minutiae of the sniper attack:

"This was a military grade weapon, accurate enough to shoot a fly's gonads off at a quarter of a mile. And it has to be somebody that knew what he was doing with a thing like that, just firing one shot."

Keith agreed. "A professional marksman, almost certainly. That's what the police seem to be saying."

"So how come such a professional fucking crack-shot hitman only got his leg?" Maz demanded to know.

"Thank the Lord he did only get his leg," Taplow replied.

"And why were there so many paramedics on hand, with all the right tackle, who just happened to be there?"

"Normal precautions for such an event," Keith answered. "Exactly what are you trying to suggest, Mr Masters?"

"I daren't even bleedin' think what I'm suggesting!"

When the tense conversation was over Taplow stroked his chin, lost in thought. It was irritating to discover that Maz wasn't as stupid as he'd wanted to believe. And certainly not as stupid as Serghei.

* * *

It was the talk of the whole country. Back in 1980 the big question on everybody's lips was, 'Who shot JR?', but that paled into insignificance next to the nationwide furore over 'Who shot Serghei?'. Extreme-right pub philosophers, who, incidentally, were all ardent supporters of the Spirit of the Nation, seemed to universally blame the Russians. There appeared to be three reasons for this school of little thought. Firstly, Russkies have always been lefties, so anti-anybody right-leaning. Secondly, don't they always interfere in elections? And thirdly they are an easy and obvious target. Remember Salisbury? And if, by any remote chance, it wasn't them, then it had to be the Chinese. The same sort of lack of reasoning seemed to apply, but just delete Salisbury from the equation, and insert Wuhan.

Marginally less xenophobic, but equally wide of the mark, were the press and the broadcast news media. Of course, in reality, this was a prime example of the truth being stranger than fiction.

On that Sunday, the day after the shocking incident, television news presenters were revelling in the intrigue. On ITV, Tom Preston had foregone his precious day of rest to front the teatime bulletin. Normally the big-name stars of the news demanded weekends off with their loved ones, leaving the TV news desks vacant for the also-rans, odd-looking journalistic misfits and keen trainees. But this was the biggest story in recent months, so Preston was presiding as frontman, facing political editor June Ellis across his desk.

"Twenty-four hours on, June, and no arrest. Are the police any nearer knowing who the would-be assassin was?" asked Tom, self-importantly.

June Ellis shook her head, a grim smile playing across her lips. "The police are saying very little, which probably means they know very little at this stage. It was obviously a highly professional job by somebody who is good at covering their tracks. Interestingly no group has claimed responsibility either, so it's a bit of a mystery at the moment. And may well remain so…"

"So what does it mean for this fascinating by-election? Will it still go ahead?"

"Well of course that is the sixty-four-thousand-dollar question. Serghei's wounds are serious, but he's stable, and presumably still capable of continuing his campaign. However, he could be forgiven for thinking that a political life like this simply isn't worth the risk. My guess would be that if Serghei pulls out they will probably postpone the election out of respect. But, interestingly, if you look at the latest polls, his popularity has surged dramatically."

"A sympathy vote…?" suggested Tom.

June nodded. "You could look at it that way. A martyr to the cause, if you like."

Tom Preston leaned forward on his desk, hands clasped together. "So… and of course I'm not wishing to trivialise the brutality of what has happened to him… but it has ironically been the best thing that could have happened?"

June agreed, without hesitation, "Purely in terms of winning the election, most definitely, yes."

"So could he win?"

"Yes. If the polls are anything to go by, and we do know from bitter experience that the polls can be extremely misleading, but yes, the suggestion is that he would now be the front-runner by quite some way."

Tom sat back and mused, "Interesting times. Thank you, June Ellis, very much indeed."

* * *

Monday morning and Serghei was sitting up in bed. Industrial-strength painkillers were allowing him to almost enjoy the attention and universal sympathy. His private hospital room was festooned with wall-to-wall flowers and hundreds of 'get well' cards, with sacks more still arriving. Maz was pacing up and down, clearly more agitated than Serghei.

"I can't believe you are even thinking about sticking with the Spirit of the Nazis and going through with this bloody election."

Serghei shrugged. "I'm not thinking about it – I'm doing it."

Maz looked at him in disbelief. "Don't you think God might have been trying to tell you something when you got your leg shot to fuck?"

"Have you seen all these flowers and cards?" asked Serghei, evading the question. "They say I am more popular now than the Beatles were. And John Lennon said they were more popular than Jesus."

Maz turned away and sighed to himself, "Houston – the ego has landed!"

But Serghei hadn't finished. "The hospital stopped counting the phone messages when they reached ten thousand."

"Don't worry," said Maz. "If you call off the election you don't have to send back the flowers."

"They say I can definitely win this."

"Any idiot can become an MP!" snapped Maz. "Have you ever seen a fuckwit called Neil Hamilton?"

* * *

A couple of days later, ITN political correspondent June Ellis was in that same hospital room with her news cameraman. The nurses had managed to get Serghei off his bed and into a wheelchair for the interview. Maz, despite his extreme misgivings, had managed to get a silk dressing gown monogrammed in time for Serghei to wear. If his boy insisted on going through with this, then they had to do it properly, in style.

The cameraman faffed around with the blinds on the window, trying to get the available lighting right, while June clipped a microphone onto Serghei's dressing gown.

With Maz watching on anxiously, June began her big exclusive:

"I think nobody would have blamed you for pulling out of this by-election, in view of what happened on Saturday. What is making you carry on?"

Serghei moved a little so that he could wince dramatically at the pain it caused. "Somebody with a lot of money has tried to silence me. If I am such a threat to the old world order, which makes the rich richer and keeps the ordinary working woman or man in their place, then I think I owe it to the ordinary working woman or man to persevere. You see I promise change, but the last thing the old order want is real change. They pretend they do, but it suits them all to swap control every few years, a fraction to the right, then a fraction to the left, but all maintaining simmering tension between bosses and their workers, to distract us from the fact that they are making life easy for themselves and lining their own pockets in the process."

June feigned shock. "So you are saying one of our main political parties was behind the shooting?"

"I'm not accusing any single person or group of people of anything, but you have to consider who would have the most to gain by me being silenced."

June raised her eyebrows, allowing the viewers to answer Serghei's question for themselves. "So what is it that are you offering that has got the other parties so rattled?"

"I think ordinary people are sick and tired of being told what they aren't allowed to think, or what they aren't allowed to say, and what they can't eat, what they can't drink, what they can't do. I think they are fed up with successive governments who care more about gender-neutral lavatories, same-sex marriage and misguided political correctness than they care about the sick, the elderly and the homeless. Aren't we all disgusted that the criminal now has more rights in law than their victim? And people are fed up of being told they generate too much land-fill rubbish when it's the supermarkets who wrap everything in plastic three times over. Don't tell an old lady it's her fault that the planet is choking to death because she hasn't recycled a yoghurt pot, when there are greedy corporations poisoning the sea and the air with billions of tons of toxic waste every single day. Let's get our priorities sorted out. It's time there was some proper perspective in British politics. We've had enough! We aren't supposed to serve the government – they are supposed to serve us. A vote for me is a vote for the common man… a vote for common sense… and a vote for God…"

The remainder of his unfinished speech from Saturday had come in handy after all.

Serghei quite enjoyed the fact that he could use his hospitalisation as a legitimate excuse for ducking any pre-election duties that didn't sound appealing, and he positively revelled in the tsunami of sympathy and love that it brought. When he finally was allowed to venture out of his room he was pushed around the streets of towns all over North Riding, in a wheelchair, to even louder cheers, yet more adulation, even tears of joy. That ego massage was more of a balm than all the morphine he'd been injected with in hospital. His incapacity also quite suited him, in that it curtailed certain less pleasant photo opportunities – namely kissing babies and pressing the flesh with total strangers.

Maz offered no resistance. What was the point? He never shared his darkest suspicions with Serghei either. He almost didn't dare to vocalise them, or even believe them himself, and he didn't have a shred of evidence. Who would believe him?

Stanley 'Maz' Masters had grown up a lonely, unloved and occasionally physically abused only-child in a rough area of London, where he'd had to acquire certain survival tactics, not to mention a rough, tough resilience. Eventually he'd done well for himself, after a good deal of ducking and diving. Entering middle age, however, he'd had to face the harsh reality that he'd never in his life had a friend. Not a real friend. Of course there were drinking buddies and work associates he'd had a laugh with, but he'd never felt close to anybody, not ever. Even girlfriends had been fleeting affairs of lust rather than love. He was beginning to realise that Serghei, infuriating and frustrating as he undoubtedly could be at times, had become like a younger brother to him. Somebody to look out for and, though he'd never dare admit it, even to himself – love.

In so many respects they were peas in a pod. Certainly their survival instincts were similar, as was their insular self-sufficiency. In rare off-guard moments they had shared memories of frighteningly similar traumas from their childhoods, which had given them both that fire in the belly to crawl out of the gutter and a hunger to prove themselves to the world. Maz had no idea where this latest venture was leading, but then he'd always said that anybody who tells you they always had a plan for the way their life panned out is a liar. What Maz was good at, and it seemed Serghei as well, was rolling with whatever life throws at you, and grabbing every opportunity with both hands. So what was the point of rocking this new boat? Deep down he also had to admit to himself that there was something in the pit of his stomach that found all this quite exciting.

CHAPTER TWENTY-TWO

It was early on the morning after the by-election. The town hall of the largest town in North Riding, where the ballot counting had gone on right through the night, was buzzing with crowds of people, assembled to hear the results. It seemed like the whole of the news media had descended upon this previously anonymous, unexceptional, right-leaning, north-eastern constituency. There were TV cameras and reporters everywhere, and photographers jockeying for the best vantage point to capture the moments of triumph and defeat, elation and tears.

There was a frisson of excitement and anticipation in the air as the candidates filed into the large hall and made their way onto the stage. The council were not as forward-thinking as some, regarding access, so they'd had to bring in a special lift to get Serghei's wheelchair up on to the platform. Fortunately, they parked him at one end of the line-up, where he wasn't masked from the cameras, and was a respectable distance away from the obligatory grinning imbecile candidate in the purple tartan trousers, red fur coat, tall yellow stovepipe hat, and a stuffed green parrot on his shoulder.

The gathered crowd fell silent as the elegantly dressed returning officer made her way forward to the lectern and the bank of microphones. She looked slightly nervous and cleared her throat a couple of times as she arranged her notes in front of her.

"I, Jill Foster, being the acting returning officer for the North Riding constituency, do hereby give notice that the total number of votes recorded for each candidate, at the said election, was as follows:

Jennifer Louise Morgan, Green Party, four hundred and

eighty-three votes."

There was a smattering of polite applause.

"Sashir Akeem Sadri, Liberal Democrat Party, one thousand eight hundred and two votes."

Another ripple from the crowd came after each of the less interesting also-rans.

"Stephen Arthur Giles, Independent, two hundred and twelve votes… Izzy Wizzy Let's Get Busy Gladstone Churchill Disraeli Smith, Monster Raving Loony Party, thirty-one votes…"

There was a small, almost embarrassed chuckle as the bizarrely dressed buffoon waved frantically with a massive foam rubber hand, moulded into a 'victory' sign.

"Roisin Marie Featherstone, Labour Party, eight thousand seven hundred and sixty-seven votes… Serghei Iliescu, Spirit of the Nation Party, twenty-nine thousand eight hundred and ninety-five votes…"

This time the gathered audience was ignited into wild applause and cheers.

"Susan Heather Williamson, Independent, ninety-two votes… Helen Elizabeth Christina Scott, Conservative Party, eleven thousand five hundred and twenty-one votes…"

At this news the crowd went crazy. Serghei had trounced the Tory candidate. It was a while before Jill Foster was able to make herself heard again.

"Therefore I give public notice that Serghei Iliescu is duly elected as Member of Parliament for the North Riding constituency."

The audience went wild once again.

* * *

Lindsey Montgomery was up before her flatmate Shanice, watching the declaration live from the North Riding on BBC Breakfast.

She put her hand to her mouth in horror and disbelief. "Oh sweet Jesus! It's really happening."

The BBC cut back to the studio for an initial comment from their morning presenters, who then linked across to their colleague who was live in the North Riding town hall for an animated chat.

The coverage then cut back to the stage where an elated Serghei was finishing his acceptance speech, which he had been given to learn the previous day: "… This is just the beginning. The beginning of a new era in British politics. And the beginning of the end for the old smug self-serving politicians with their greed, half-truths and humbug. The beginning of an era where, with God's help, we put the Great back into Britain. Thank you all! Are we ready for change?"

The crowd went berserk, surging forward, cheering and chanting in response. People were jostling and pushing to get close to Serghei and take a photo, some reaching up in a vain attempt to touch their new redeemer. Maz wasn't at all sure whether he was pleased or not with the result, but he was decidedly pissed off as, unrecognised, he got callously and roughly shoved and elbowed out of the way by the heaving throng of people. He fought his way to the back of the room and stood alone, watching the mania unfold in front of him. Serghei was theirs now. Had Maz lost him?

*　*　*

Sir George Henderson had been at home watching the same live BBC coverage as Lindsey, but, as you would expect, reacted to it rather differently. It would have been unseemly to leap up and down shouting and screaming, but, in his head, he had been doing exactly that.

Keith Taplow, who had been staying up in the North Riding all week, spent the day massaging Serghei's ego and overseeing the riotous celebrations. After which he spent a good deal of time motivating, congratulating and inspiring the faithful party workers, following this tremendous victory. As he said to them, this was just the beginning.

That evening he had been driven down from the north east directly to Sir George's Surrey mansion and had been ushered by the incongruously feminine butler into the elegant, oak-panelled drawing-room. The two men were now seated in high-backed leather armchairs, enjoying the warmth radiating from a blazing log fire and staring contentedly into the flickering flames. Another of Sir George's unobtrusive, yet glamorous home-helps was pouring vintage Champagne for them. It was something very special from the cellar, but this was, without doubt, the most momentous occasion.

Sir George picked up his lead crystal Champagne flute and delicately sniffed the almost priceless liquid. With his left hand he then lifted the bottle from the solid silver ice bucket on its matching stand and looked lovingly at the label.

"Boerl and Kroff. An exceptional year, apparently. I have been saving this for a special occasion. And I think occasions don't come any more special than this." He raised his glass. "To our Romanian saviour!"

Keith hesitated, "Let's not give him too much of the credit."

Sir George smiled enigmatically. "Ah, we are all so big, and yet so small."

Taplow raised his own Champagne flute, deep in thought, and proposed an alternative toast. "To a day I wasn't sure we'd ever live to see."

"A day to end all days," Sir George agreed, accepting the toast and raising his glass.

They sipped the exorbitantly priced fizz and sat quietly for a while, savouring both the moment and the velvety vintage Champagne.

Eventually Sir George broke the contented silence. "Much to be done, dear boy. We'll never get this close again. Mustn't lose the momentum."

Taplow nodded in agreement. "We're ready. And today's morale boost has got everybody all fired up."

"Make the most of this honeymoon period. Rose-tinted spectacles and victory blinkers will stop the great unwashed seeing what is happening. For now."

Taplow nodded again, "The wheels are already in motion."

"There will be a backlash at some point," Sir George added gravely. "The media will turn. Some of them at least."

"Collins has his Neanderthals primed."

Sir George, on being reminded about the sometimes unpleasant realities of the road to success, suddenly asked, "Have they caught anybody for the shooting yet?"

"They arrested some psycho this morning, after a tip-off. Story got nicely lost in the maelstrom of the election victory."

"And did he do it?"

Keith shook his head. "No. But he had the gun that did, so he'll go down for it. The police just love a happy ending."

Sir George put up a hand to stop Keith saying any more. "I said I wouldn't ask."

There was another amicable silence while they sipped their Champagne.

"Are the funds in place?" asked Keith. "It's going to be a very costly few months."

"I'm beating donors, who wish to remain anonymous, away with a hefty stick. You'd be very surprised if I were to tell you where the really big money is coming from. But that would be careless talk. Just rest assured it's there."

Keith nodded and looked thoughtfully into his glass. "Which just leaves us with the Masters problem."

Sir George frowned slightly and looked up. "I know you don't like the man, but tread very carefully. You must consider whether he is a lot more than merely a thorn in our sides. Without his Svengali pulling the strings our priceless puppet might just collapse lifeless on the floor. And that, my dear Keith, would be unthinkable…"

* * *

Serghei stumbled and collapsed on the floor. He was far from lifeless though, growling loudly in pain and anger. It was about three weeks after the by-election and ten days after his reconstructive knee surgery, in a large physiotherapy room, back home in London. The patient physiotherapist helped a frustrated and ill-tempered Serghei back to his feet.

"Rome wasn't built in a day, Mr Iliescu. Baby steps, baby steps. Literally, to start with."

Serghei winced in agony as he straightened up, exclaiming loudly, "La naiba! Pula mea!"

Maz, who had been anxiously watching from the side of the room, quickly stepped in. "Oh shit. The right honourable gentleman is swearing in Romanian. That's never a good thing. Give us a minute, darling."

The physio hesitated then shrugged and walked out.

Maz held Serghei's arm for support. "Don't give that poor cow a hard time – she didn't shoot you! Although if you don't sort your attitude she might go get a gun and take your other fucking knee out! And, frankly, I wouldn't grass her up if she did."

"It fucking hurts!" growled Serghei.

"I'm sure it does." Maz's tone softened as he helped Serghei to a chair. "Look, they said you might never walk again, and you're gonna prove 'em wrong, champ. Another Serghei miracle. Your adoring public will love it. Who do you want to give it to? Jonathan Ross? Graham Norton? They'll snap your bleedin' arm off!"

"I'll ask Keith what he thinks."

Maz closed his eyes in despair, but bit his tongue.

* * *

Lindsey hadn't given up the fight. Once again she and Clive were in their favourite wine bar, Wonderland. It was getting harder and harder to keep Clive on side, but she still believed his knowledge of magic made him a good ally.

"But surely we're too late," said Clive, in answer to Lindsey's rallying cry. "I don't see any point. He's already got everything he wants."

Lindsey shook her head. "I have a horrible feeling this is just the beginning. There's something going on. It's like bloody Trump all over again."

"Well what can we do about it? Two lost voices, out of step with the masses."

"We have to try. There are lots of others out there, it's not only us. We just have to galvanise them."

Clive didn't look convinced. "But I'm just a magician. All I wanted to do was prove that he was just a magician as well, and his so-called God-given mystical powers were no more miracles than some red-nosed dodgy clown at a kids' party pulling a moth-eaten rabbit out of a hat."

Lindsey agreed. "Don't you see? That's the point. That's still his Achilles heel. Everything he has built up has been based on a foundation of lies. If we could finally expose him, convince people he's been conning them all along…"

"They don't want to know the truth. They never have. It's like a six-year-old doesn't want to know that Santa Claus is just his mum."

Lindsey stood firm. "Then we have to convince them."

Clive let out a weary sigh. "I don't know. I'm out of my depth here. Anyway it's like everybody has forgotten how he became famous. He doesn't really do his magic stuff any more."

Lindsey looked thoughtful. "The media won't let him forget. They'll want him to perform. His vanity will get the better of him sooner or later."

CHAPTER TWENTY-THREE

Lindsey Montgomery was certainly right about one thing. This was just the beginning. Within a month of the by-election, with Serghei now a serving MP, only the second ever to represent the Spirit of the Nation Party in the House of Commons, news broke of the resignation of Rupert Forsythe.

ITN's Tom Preston was full of it on *News at Ten*. Against archive shots of Forsythe grinning from ear to ear and swilling down a pint of beer in a pub, just before the last general election, the newsman could barely disguise his glee as he announced:

"The big story tonight is the surprise resignation of the leader of the Spirit of the Nation Party, Rupert Forsythe. In a press statement issued by party headquarters at ten o'clock this morning, they cited that old chestnut 'personal reasons', and said that his successor would be their new Member of Parliament, Serghei Iliescu. Mister Forsythe had this to say, earlier this afternoon…"

The director then cut to a shot of the media scrum outside Forsythe's posh looking country home, earlier that day. The wide gate across the gravel drive was firmly locked, holding back the baying journalists, photographers and cameramen, but Forsythe had wheeled his wife out of the safety of their home, for moral support. Hand in hand they were leaning on the gate, desperately trying to look as though this was the best day of their lives, rather than the worst. Forcing a smile, Forsythe gave this statement:

"I have devoted seven years to creating a brand-new party from scratch, building a following, through getting our first MP into the House, a party name change, then this landslide of popular opinion in North Riding. That is a legacy of which I am extremely proud. But this job isn't nine to five. It defines your life. I think I've achieved a lot, and now it's time for me to reclaim my life. I know it's an old political cliché, but I really do want to spend more time with my family." He feigned a warm smile towards his spouse and asked a rhetorical, "Don't I, darling?"

She feigned a reciprocal smile and nodded, allowing her husband to continue. "I'm not leaving the party. I will continue fighting the good fight to make this nation great again."

A reporter butted in, "What about the new leader?"

It was even harder to fake a smile this time. "Oh, I think the party will be in very good hands."

He'd accomplished all the sham bonhomie he could manage on that subject, so he quickly wrapped things up. "Now that's all I have to say at this time. Thank you all for coming."

With that Rupert Forsythe turned and crunched off up the long gravel drive, leading his wife back to their marble-pillared front porch.

That might be all that the man himself had to say on the subject, but it was far from all that Tom Preston had to say:

"Rupert Forsythe, who resigned as leader of the Spirit of the Nation Party this morning. Our political editor, June Ellis joins me now. So what is really going on, June?"

June Ellis, who had joined Tom across his large news desk, was similarly revelling in the day's surprise news. "Yet another massive PR boost for the SON in actual fact. Serghei Iliescu is already the politician with the highest approval rating since they started measuring those sorts of things, and, as a result, the party itself has soared in the polls. This will surely take them to even greater heights."

Preston leaned forward on his forearms, delighting in the intrigue. "But Rupert Forsythe – did he really jump, or was he pushed?"

"A reliable inside source told me that he was, shall we say, actively encouraged to step aside."

Tom smiled. "Any specific reason? Has he had his fingers

in the till?"

"No, no, nothing like that. He served his purpose, but politics is brutal. The sideways nudge is purely to make room for his successor. I think what the party very shrewdly have done today is to cash in on Serghei Iliescu's mass national popularity, dare I say 'adulation', in an attempt to spread his success way beyond North Riding."

Tom, for added dramatic effect, referred to the notes in front of him. "Interestingly the SON didn't call Mr Iliescu 'acting' leader in the press statement the party issued earlier today, which would be normal under these circumstances."

June shook her head. "No, no. He's leader."

Preston raised an eyebrow. "Can they do that without a leadership contest?"

"They just have!" June grinned. "Look, a party can do whatever it wants, within its own rulebook, and they can even change the rules if necessary. Traditionally parties don't do things like this for fear of upsetting the party faithful, but these are extraordinary political times, as we saw not too long ago in America, and here with Brexit. In this case the party faithful are smart enough to realise that Mr Iliescu is the best thing to happen to the party since the day it was created as the BIP, so why rock the boat?"

Tom leaned in again, more seriously this time. "There isn't a general election due for nearly two years, so is this astonishing flash-in-the-pan really a threat to the old two-party system?"

"I think it is in a way. There has been a lot of very bloody in-fighting amongst Conservatives in recent years, and even more so within the perennially fractured Labour Party. Nothing seduces politicians more than opportunism, success, and popularity, so I think we should expect defections from all the major parties to the Spirit of the Nation."

Tom raised the other eyebrow. "On a grand scale?"

"Who knows? Possibly so, yes."

Tom smiled wryly and shook his head. "Extraordinary times. June Ellis, thank you very much indeed."

* * *

Lindsey reacted to the shocking news immediately. After the ten o'clock bulletin ended she went to her bedroom and set up her laptop computer to record a vlog entry. She diligently checked the background of the shot. She didn't want anybody being distracted by discarded clothing or a crumpled duvet.

"Hi. Lindsey Montgomery here. We are currently living through an era where the watchword seems to be 'hysteria'. We get hysterical about everything, from public outpourings of grief for people we've never even met, to hysteria about taking offence over things that really don't concern us. And the one I really don't understand is the hysteria over 'C-list' celebrities. Haven't we learned anything from America? 'C-list' celebrities don't make great politicians. I know we are all fed up with these slick, smarmy, career politicians, but at least they do know how the system works. Just because somebody is a bit famous it doesn't make them good at everything. You might not like smart aleck patronising garage mechanics, but who would you rather fixed the faulty brakes on your car? Two qualified, but irritating clever-dicks from your local Kwik-Fit, or the Chuckle Brothers? Actually I shouldn't make a joke out of this. It's serious. Serghei Iliescu is a hugely popular magician. And that's all he is. A good conjuror. He doesn't have mystical God-given powers. He's lied continuously about that. And, other than his undeniable talents as a liar, he has no qualifications whatsoever to be in politics. So what is really scary is that I believe he is probably just being used as a frontman – the acceptable face of far-right extremism."

Forty-eight hours later, she was standing by her desk in the newspaper office, sulkily tossing her personal effects into one of those cardboard storage boxes that you usually only see in Hollywood movies, when somebody gets fired. Her boss, Derek Hyland, was standing watching her, with his hands on his hips. He was speaking. She was pretending not to listen. She certainly wasn't dignifying anything he was saying with a response. Although the odd tut or occasional sigh betrayed the fact that she was taking it all in, albeit reluctantly.

"You can't say I didn't warn you Lindsey. I said, the first sign of conflict of interest. You knew our corporate stance on Serghei. Sir George is absolutely apoplectic. He wanted your head on a pole by the lifts as a warning to the others. So, for obvious reasons, you're going to really struggle to get another job in London."

Derek watched Lindsey toss the mouse mat from her computer into the box. He reached in to retrieve it. "The mouse mat is ours. Look, if I was you, I'd disappear off to the *Harrogate Herald* and have a couple of years reporting on car crashes, coffee mornings and fly-tipping. Then, when we see which way all this goes, you just might – MIGHT – be able to sneak back in through the back door."

Lindsey picked up her cardboard box and flounced off towards the lifts, without saying a word, or looking back.

* * *

Maz had been alone when he saw the first breaking news bulletin about Serghei being declared leader of the Spirit of the Nation Party, and he couldn't help himself. He laughed until the tears rolled down his cheeks. How had it come to this bizarre state of affairs? Of course he had known exactly what was going to happen and when. It had all been planned for weeks. He was also fully aware of all the Machiavellian machinations that had gone on behind the scenes to get to that point, but the reality of it all only really struck him when he saw it right there in front of him on the television news. He almost reached the point of hysteria as he sat alone, giggling uncontrollably.

It wasn't particularly what he'd wanted, but Sir George and Keith had successfully wooed Serghei, so he'd reluctantly gone along with the whole thing. Ever the pragmatist, Maz had thrown himself whole-heartedly into backing Serghei and doing whatever needed doing. And, it has to be said, the tax-free 'expenses' from the party were extremely generous, and the unofficial perks were mind-boggling. The party stalwarts clearly did recognise Maz's fundamental importance as a Svengali figure.

When he eventually stopped laughing he phoned Serghei saying that he was hopping in a cab to his place so that they could get hopelessly wasted together to celebrate, which is precisely what they did. They say good Champagne doesn't leave you with a hangover, but they made damned sure that they drunk enough of it to guarantee that, when they regained consciousness the next morning, they both had eyes like clumsily fried eggs, and heads pounding like the anvils of two blacksmiths on steroids.

* * *

With this sudden and extensive flurry of interest in the Spirit of the Nation, sleeping giants started to awaken. Questions were being asked in more serious circles regarding Serghei's lack of experience and knowledge of the world of politics, and what policies the party would campaign on in any future elections. Their chequered history as the British Independent Party hadn't been completely forgotten, and neither had their far-right tendencies and doctrines.

A shrewd strategy had been formulated whereby their more extreme views were played down, in favour of more people-pleasing promises and aspirations. Another tactic was employed, which had proved successful for Donald J Trump, amongst others. The goal was to touch as many raw nerves as possible with the ordinary woman or man in the street, by listing all their greatest fears, paranoia and niggles, together with all the scary problems of the wider world, so that they would feel included and recognised, agreeing, "Yes, that's exactly what's wrong with my life!" That made it sound as though there was some intention to do something about all these things. The truth didn't necessarily have to match the suppositions made, and no actual promises had been given, so none were going to be broken. It's a smart way of getting people onside.

Nevertheless, the party officials all realised that Serghei needed briefing and preparing for his new role, as he was going to have to face some tougher questions than had been posed previously by *Hello* magazine, and *The One Show*.

CHAPTER TWENTY-FOUR

Maz, the man with an extremely important role, yet no job description, was in his office doing whatever needed to be done for this daunting new venture. He told Kat, his PA, that he wasn't to be disturbed for the next twenty minutes as he had a private and confidential phone call to make.

When she had left he took out a notepad and a pen, then pulled a scrap of paper out of his pocket with a landline phone number written on it. Out of another pocket he withdrew an old mobile phone. It was one of those small Japanese handsets which predated smartphones and large touch screens. It had real buttons with numbers on them, which peeped when pressed. Glancing at the scrap of paper he pushed the appropriate buttons and waited for an answer. It took quite a while for the elderly lady to get to the phone, but she did pick up eventually.

"Good morning, my love," schmoozed Maz in a surprisingly warm and agreeable tone. "Oh, now you've got a lovely, friendly voice. That's just what I need. Nobody wants to talk to me today."

He let her answer.

"I know. I'll be getting the sack if I don't get somebody to talk to me pretty soon."

He had cleverly appealed to her kind nature and she said she didn't want him getting sacked, so she'd be happy to talk to him. In truth she was all alone and any human voice was a break from the monotony of her lonely solitude.

"That's very sweet of you, my darling. Well I wonder if you could possibly spare me a few minutes just to answer a short survey for me. It's about insurance, but there's no pressure to buy anything, I promise you. I just need you to answer a few questions."

Again the sweet old lady agreed.

"Oh that's ever so kind of you. You know what, darling? I could tell you sounded lovely the minute you picked up the phone. First of all, do you mind telling me what kind of car you drive? … Oh, you don't drive… What about your husband? … Oh I'm so sorry to hear that… Do you mind me asking how?"

The lady spent a few emotional moments recounting the sad passing of her husband just six months ago, whilst in hospital being treated for a stroke. They had said he'd recover, but something went wrong in the Intensive Care Unit and he never came home.

Maz started making copious notes, before gently steering her back onto the subject of driving, as this was an insurance survey after all.

"So your husband used to do all the driving. Where was your favourite place he used to take you?"

He continued to furiously scribble down everything she divulged.

"Do you by any chance have a son or a daughter who has a car? … Right, what sort of car has he got? … Oh! Very snazzy! He's doing well for himself. You must be very proud of him. Does he take you out for drives in that? … He does? … Where does he take you? … That's lovely. What a nice son you've got. You brought him up well, darling. Did you send him to private school? … Oh really?"

And so the questioning went on, until Maz had everything he needed, all jotted down on the pad in front of him. He thanked the elderly lady profusely for all her time and trouble, promising that he wouldn't bother her again. He then wound up the call, pocketing the phone and secreting the notepad, together with the lady's number, in his lockable briefcase. Maz sat there for a few moments looking pleased with himself before he asked Kat to book him a car to take him to Serghei's apartment.

* * *

Chatham was an eponymously named weekly television programme, which unflinchingly analysed and dissected current affairs and serious issues of the day. Jeremy Chatham was an intelligent, tough-talking journalist who had a reputation for giving politicians a hard time when he interrogated them. Many quite senior political figures, even cabinet ministers, were too cowardly to face him. Inevitably the Spirit of the Nation received an invitation for their new leader to be grilled by Mr Chatham. Had they declined it would have been seen as weakness – and they were promising strength.

Serghei had been extensively coached and primed for this important cross-examination for days, but Keith Taplow still worried that this veteran intimidating interviewer might expose the undeniable chinks in their new party leader's armour.

That week's programme featured a heated debate between a senior minister and his feisty Labour counterpart on the opposition's proposal of tax rises for the wealthy, in order to escape the austerity measures introduced by the unfeeling Tory government; plus, a film on escalating tensions in Iran. The hard-nosed host's interview with Serghei was to be the conclusion of the show.

The name *Chatham* was emblazoned in large letters across the back of the studio set, and the two protagonists were picked out in stark pools of light to emphasise the unforgiving nature of the interview. Serghei was sitting in his wheelchair facing his formidable adversary as the floor manager counted out of the Iran film and into the final part of this live forty-five-minute broadcast. Far more people than normal were tuning in to this somewhat earnest programme, purely to see the darling of the nation. An awful lot was riding on this encounter.

"With me now is Serghei Iliescu, the recently appointed leader of the Spirit of the Nation Party. Welcome, Mr Iliescu. I think the public at large, and especially us journalists, have to acknowledge that you have been like a breath of fresh air in British politics, and you are undoubtedly a charismatic entertainer, but is it daunting now that it's all getting a bit serious?"

It was a soft start, but that didn't necessarily bode well.

Serghei picked up on the veiled dig. "It has always been serious. I didn't go into this lightly. I think it is time British politics was given a bit of a shake-up. They – the old guard from Labour and Conservative – with their apathy and arrogance, as we saw earlier in your programme, have almost destroyed a previously great nation."

Chatham leaned forward, "But your party has some 'robust' policies which a lot of liberal-minded voters find, at the very least, unsettling. The SON website talks about a 'repatriation programme', for example."

"That would be purely voluntary. We would help anybody wishing to return to their families or country of origin. There are lots of people who would love to return to their roots, but simply can't afford to do so."

Jeremy Chatham frowned. "So nobody would be forced or coerced into repatriation?"

"Of course not."

"You see some people might argue that those kind of policies seem a bit ironic as your own roots are from overseas."

"But I am happy to stay here. I am a British citizen. I choose to stay. You know, that is what has always made Britain great. Decent people from other countries with talent and a good work ethic have always been embraced here. Historically Britain is probably the world's finest example of a true melting-pot. What are you? Anglo-Saxon? Celtic? Norman? Roman? Viking? Jewish? A bit of everything?"

The host changed the subject. "So you have a real ambition to be Prime Minister?"

Serghei cleverly looked almost perplexed by the question. "Of course. Why not?"

"Isn't the problem that when the razzmatazz and the ballyhoo all dies down, which it inevitably will, there is a serious job to be done. Are you really up to that most important of tasks?"

Serghei wasn't rising to the antagonistic bait. "Listen, I have observed every Prime Minister, every US President, take office full of smiles, big promises and optimism, and, after six months, they age ten years and adopt that haunted look that says, 'Help, Mum! This job is a lot tougher than I realised, so I'll just let everything coast along towards the edge of the precipice like it always has'. I am going into this with my eyes wide open. There will be resistance, but there will be change – real change."

Things were going too well, so Chatham twisted the knife. "High ideals are all very well, but what do you know about the realities of economy and finance, nuclear defence, our place in NATO, and our ongoing trade relationship with Europe and China?"

Serghei remained unfazed, these were still the type of questions he had been coached to handle. "You know, a weak leader puts weak people under him or her, so that they are no threat to their fragile leadership. A great leader isn't afraid to have strong people in the wings, and I have the greatest, and I mean the greatest team behind me."

The no-nonsense journalist wasn't letting him off the hook so easily. "But a leader must have his own personal views on critical issues. What is your take, for example, on benefits? And unsustainable pensions, with an increasingly older population growing in number and age every day?"

Serghei began to look a little uncomfortable, for the first time.

Chatham spotted this and kept jabbing. "A National Health Service which is quite clearly falling apart at the seams, and the current very real crisis in healthcare for the elderly. What answers have you got for them?"

Serghei's eyes flickered, as though the hand of God had just touched him. "These are issues that worry you, yes?"

The host sat back, feigning shock. "They are issues that worry everybody, surely."

It was Serghei's turn to lean forward, fixing Chatham with an intense stare. "But you have a deeply personal interest. It is your mother, right? She is alone. In a care home – no, alone at home with a carer who calls. Your father passed away in hospital. Oh, I'm sorry, it is only six months ago. He'd had a stroke, but you blame the hospital, don't you?"

Jeremy looked a little unsettled. "That's not really... This is personal stuff that I'd... I don't want to... Can we go back to my question?"

Serghei was undeterred. "What is the connection with Charles Dickens?"

Chatham was now getting flustered. "Can we just keep..."

Serghei concentrated hard. "Broadstairs in Kent. Charles Dickens called it 'our English watering place'. Why is that on your mind, I wonder? Ah, I see. Your father liked you to take him there, and now you take your mother in your open-topped white Mercedes."

"Please, this is not..." stammered the hard-nosed host. "How do you know this stuff?"

Serghei offered up a few more unsettling personal revelations, much to his interrogator's discomfort. Fortunately, their allotted time was almost at an end and Jeremy Chatham managed to flounder his way to some sort of conclusion.

* * *

The next afternoon Clive was in Wonderland, buying the drinks for a change, as Lindsey was now unemployed. When they sat at their usual table Lindsey showed Clive the banner headline from her former employer's paper: *Psychic Serghei derails TV interview, leaving Chatham speechless*.

"It's a trick, right?" she asked.

Clive looked smug. "Of course it is. Magicians, mentalists, mind-readers call it 'pre-show work'. You just need somebody else to get all that personal information for you beforehand, without arousing suspicion. It's how the good mediums work as well."

"Then we have to expose it," said Lindsey emphatically.

Clive shrugged. "I've already uploaded a YouTube clip on my page, but I'm not sure anybody will take the slightest bit of notice. They don't want to see him discredited – especially now he's in a sodding wheelchair."

Lindsey ignored his negativity, "I'll put something on my blog, try drive some traffic to your page. The blog is beginning to gain momentum. Twenty thousand views yesterday. At long last right-minded people are waking up to what's going on here. We must keep chipping away. Who do you think supplied the information about Chatham?"

"His mother most likely. Serghei won't have contacted her himself, of course. He's too smart for that, but one of his cronies will have been in touch with her in the past week or so."

Lindsey nodded. "Okay – I'll get in touch with the mother, see if she remembers any odd calls last week. Do you want another Malbec?"

"I'd better get them," offered Clive. "What are you living on at the moment, anyway?"

Lindsey smiled a grim smile. "I start tomorrow night in a bar, just to pay the bills until I work out what to do. You see I think if the press turns against Serghei I'll be able to write my own meal ticket."

Clive looked shocked. "Is that all this is now? A crusade to further your own career?"

"That's not fair, Clive. I lost a perfectly good job because I feel so strongly about all this."

He immediately backed off. "Yeh, sorry, it's just I'm beginning to feel way out of my depth here. I have to be certain I'm doing this for the right reasons."

Lindsey smiled reassuringly. "Of course you are. We both are."

CHAPTER TWENTY-FIVE

Keith Taplow was sitting in the back of Sir George's chauffeur-driven Rolls Royce, travelling with Sir George to party headquarters to rally the troops and hold a strategy meeting. They were driving along The Mall and had timed it badly. It was the daily changing of the Horse Guards, which, whilst a spectacular bit of pageantry for visitors and tourists, was a minor inconvenience to traffic in that part of London every morning. The two men looked out of the car at the immaculately groomed horses, each bearing an imposingly upright guard in his spotless red dress uniform. The sun was glinting on their silver helmets and breast plates, making a stirring sight. If nothing else it served to remind them of the glory days of the Empire and Britain's military might.

As the chauffeur patiently waited for the parade to move along, Sir George turned to Keith and asked, "How long before we could be ready for a general election?"

"We've got two years. We'll be ready."

Sir George shook his head. "We don't have two years. This moment will never happen again. In two years the national hysteria will have died down and our golden goose will have lost his lustre. He did well with that Chatham fellow the other night, but he can't keep avoiding the difficult questions for ever. The rival broadsheets are beginning to take an interest, and it will take more than a bent spoon to sway a damning editorial. I give it nine months. Less than a year at any rate."

Keith looked perplexed. "But there won't be an election in that time."

Sir George let one of his enigmatic smiles play across his lips. "Oh, but there might be. Let's just say there's an election six months from now. Could we be ready?"

"It would be tight, but yes, I think so. Nothing makes things move faster than an imposed deadline."

Sir George nodded gravely. "We'd need to get Collins' Neanderthals involved. A spate of civil unrest. Riots. Racial tension. A handful of strikes that never seem to end. We can dig up some tragic tales that prove the NHS is in terminal decline. Revive the MPs' expenses scandal. It's never really gone away, they've just got more careful, but we can soon unearth a few prominent Tory sacrificial lambs. We engineer a factory closure that makes a whole town unemployed and then we hit the government with a 'vote of no confidence'. Lo and behold – a snap election."

Keith considered the implications for a moment. "We've got hundreds of thousands of fake social media accounts ready and waiting to spread the word, and I've got a few tame back-benchers standing by for the right moment to cross the floor of the house. That can happen right away. Start sowing the seed."

Sir George looked pleased with Taplow's positive response. "Yes, the sooner the better. And any dissenters, like cockroaches, stamp on them before they rock the boat. Stamp on them hard!"

* * *

Lindsey was in the noisy hot kitchen behind the bar where she'd taken the temporary job. She'd managed to find a corner where she could just about make a phone call, far enough away from the shouting, the clanking pans and flaming woks. Her call had gone to voicemail, so she was leaving a long convoluted message:

"Clive – it's me again, Lindsey. This is my third message. Not sure why you're not replying. Get back to me please. Your YouTube page seems to have gone down, and I can't even find your website, or your Facebook, come to that. What's happening? Hope you haven't lost your nerve. What we are doing is making a difference."

Just then there was an irritated shout through the door from the head barman, "Come on Lindsey – get off your phone! There are people out here dying of thirst!"

Lindsey pulled a face, then continued with her message, talking slightly faster. "I traced Chatham's mother, but that's a lost cause, I'm afraid. She can't remember who she spoke to ten minutes ago, never mind last week, and, bless her, she thinks she spoke to her dead husband this morning, so she's not going to prove to be a key witness. I even managed to get hold of her phone records. There was a longish call from a pay-as-you-go phone about a week ago. That was almost certainly the one, but it's untraceable, goddammit."

There was a now irate yell from the bar, "Lindsey!"

"Got to go! Call me…"

The next morning, still having had no response from Clive, Lindsey was in West Ruislip, repeatedly pressing the musical door chime and banging on the door of his flat. She was relieved to hear the door chain being slipped into place and the lock being turned. The door opened a crack and Molly peered out suspiciously.

"Mrs Entwhistle – is Clive in by any chance?"

"Who are you?" Molly demanded to know, in a small quavering voice.

Lindsey realised that Molly looked upset, so she reassured her that she was a friend who was worried about Clive.

A few minutes later they were sitting on the sofa, having a nice cup of tea. Lindsey had a comforting arm around a tearful Molly.

"I phoned the police when he didn't come home," wept Molly. "They made out like I was wasting their time. They says he's thirty-six, he's probably off gallivantin' somewhere, but I know him – he'd never do that, not without letting me know. It's two days now."

Lindsey gave her a gentle squeeze. "I'll try tracing his phone."

Molly shook her head. "It just rings and goes to his answering machine."

"But you can trace smartphones with GPS."

Molly looked dubious, "I can't be doing with any of that malarkey. All seems a bit like mumbo-jumbo if you ask me. But I'm seeing a psychic tomorrow…"

* * *

Maz looked all around in disbelief. He'd heard the saying 'how the other half live', but this was how the other miniscule fraction of one per cent live. He was on board Sir George's forty-metre, six-berth Sunseeker yacht, valued, with one careful owner, in the region of seventeen million pounds. It was moored in Salterns Marina, with spectacular views to the east of the luxury seaside resort of Sandbanks in Dorset, where property is the dearest in the whole of the United Kingdom. This was literally a billionaire's paradise.

It was a beautiful sunny day, so the walls had been opened out in the plush lounge area on the upper deck. An attractive uniformed stewardess was serving Maz and Sir George with vintage Champagne and canapes.

Sir George acknowledged Maz's obvious appreciation of their surroundings and the perfect weather. "A glorious day, Mr Masters." He then picked up his glass, and added significantly, "A glorious time."

Maz was watching the stewardess discreetly retire, leaving them in peace. He couldn't help himself, "A glorious arse."

"Mm?" Sir George looked puzzled for a fleeting moment. "Oh, indeed."

He then raised his glass, "Good health."

Maz grinned, "Bottoms up!"

You can take the boy out of the East End, but you can't take the East End out of the boy. There was a slightly uncomfortable hiatus as the two men realised how little they had in common, and what different worlds they came from.

Sir George broke the silence with shared small-talk. "Did Lizzie pick you up without any trouble?"

"Yeh. She's a diamond. Bang on the dot. Just caught up in a bit of a scrum round the Chertsey Interchange."

"Ah," nodded Sir George gravely, as though they were discussing Armageddon itself. "Chertsey Interchange."

Maz was never one for beating around the bush. "Look, let's cut to the chase, is this where you make me an offer I can't refuse? Or more likely can't survive?"

Sir George smiled amiably. "You have us all wrong. I know you and Keith don't quite see eye to eye about everything, which is why I thought you and I have should have a quiet tête-à-tête out of town. Lovely here, isn't it?"

"Yeh, it's…" Wideboy Maz was about to confect one of his typical sarcastic responses, then looked around him and found even he didn't have the cheek. "Yeh, actually it is."

"You should see the big boat in Monte Carlo. You'd definitely like that. Next time, maybe?"

They sipped Champagne in a more amicable silence this time, with Maz struggling to imagine a better boat.

"How is Serghei's leg healing?" asked Sir George suddenly, showing genuine concern, even if his motive was ulterior. "I should have asked sooner."

"Not too bad now, as it goes. He limps with all the grace of a three-legged camel, but he's up and about again. He just can't resist the sympathy so he hops back in the wheelchair for photo opps."

Sir George nodded, then stared into his glass reflectively, before saying, "We really do understand your importance in all this, Mr Masters. Mr Puppet Master."

Maz corrected him, "Serghei is a lot more than just a puppet."

"Now, now. False modesty doesn't become you, Mr Masters. Or suit you for that matter. I've observed how you operate. He dances beautifully, but only because deft hands are pulling the strings. He's smart, but you're a darned sight smarter."

Maz gave nothing away as he looked back at Sir George impassively.

His host persevered with the bonding exercise. "We have to

get through this trust barrier, Mr Masters. This is bigger than any one of us, so we all need each other. No disharmony, no hesitation."

Maz was warming to Sir George and let his guard drop a little. "Serghei's loving it all, no question. Me? I'm not so sure. This isn't what we set out to do. Actually I think it's fucking insane, if I'm honest."

Sir George raised a disapproving eyebrow. "You set out to make him a national phenomenon, right?"

Maz nodded. "Right…"

"And you achieved that in spades…"

"Right…"

"Then what's so wrong with 'global phenomenon'? That is what we are talking about here. This will rock democracy, and rock the world order. Not before time, quite frankly."

Maz stared out to sea, sipping his Champagne. If this was really that big then what the hell was he doing there in the thick of it all?

Sir George noted his uncertainty and asked, "What do you want?"

"What do you mean what do I want?" asked Maz suspiciously.

"We all have needs – some simple, some a lot more complicated, but you're in the happy position you can have just about anything your heart desires."

Maz faced up to Sir George. "You just want to buy me to get me back on-side."

Sir George shrugged. "That's about the size of it, yes."

Maz couldn't help laughing. "Bloody Nora! Well thanks for the disarming honesty."

"You have given us a Messiah, we want to reward you. Simple as that. I repeat – what do you want, Mr Masters?"

Maz relaxed a little and invited less formality. "Call me Maz."

Sir George winced and then said, with a wry smile, "That's one little thing you can't have. I don't think I could ever bring myself to call you that, Mr Masters."

CHAPTER TWENTY-SIX

Despite the apparent inevitability of each new development, Lindsey couldn't help but watch the news open-mouthed.

"The government was today rocked by a mass defection. Six Tory back-bench MPs symbolically crossed the floor of the House of Commons this morning, to join the Spirit of the Nation Party, drastically reducing the already floundering Tory party's majority, and of course the SON will be tougher opposition on many issues than Labour ever were. Serghei Iliescu said this was a great day for Britain."

Lindsey was horrified. She was still wracked with guilt about Clive's disappearance. The police had now officially listed him as a missing person, but they showed little interest in finding him. Lindsey visited his mother when she could, making reassuring noises that Clive was bound to turn up soon, but, deep down, she was far from convinced.

She kidded herself that she owed it to Clive to continue her crusade, but the truth was bigger than that. She felt she owed it to society, and she had used Clive for the greater good. It was an uncomfortable truth with which she had to live. She couldn't bring herself to think of him as cannon-fodder, but that wasn't far short of the mark.

Lindsey moved through to her bedroom and set up her laptop to record another edition of her vlog. She swallowed hard, took a deep breath, looked into the camera and pressed 'start':

"As a nation we should all be extremely concerned, but it seems we're not. There is something very worrying going on, and nobody appears to be taking it seriously. It's almost like world affairs have become a gigantic reality show, where celebrity is more important than sanity, reason, compassion and diplomacy. Have we learned nothing from America? Democracy itself is at stake here. The real danger is that the world's desire for big personalities has opened a global portal for the extreme right; a gateway to Hell, which will be hard to close. It's time for traditionally benign and moderate, right-minded, free-thinking people to unite and galvanise themselves against the current trend towards hatred and intolerance, and to stop the lunatics taking over the asylum. It's been said before, but it doesn't make it any less true – bad things happen when good people do nothing."

The next evening Lindsey returned home from a lunchtime shift at the bar, followed by another harrowing visit to see Clive's mother, who was becoming more and more distraught with worry. Lindsey looked around. The flat looked different. It was all neat, tidy and orderly, but all the furniture had been moved around into different configurations, with the TV set now facing the wall. Her flatmate Shanice, who had just returned home from work, was standing in the middle of the oddly rearranged living area, in shock.

Lindsey put her hand to her mouth, seeing her friend looking so upset. "Jesus, Shan – what's happened?"

Shanice was on the verge of tears. "I just came back. It's really creepy. Nothing's missing or broken, but everything's been moved around. What in God's name have you got yourself involved in, Lindse? I think some scary bastard's trying to say 'we know where you live!'"

Lindsey looked around in a panic, then spotted a full bowl of cat food on the floor of their kitchen area. "Oh my God, where's Bojangles?"

* * *

Over the next days and weeks, the news bulletins kept coming thick and fast, pretty much as Sir George Henderson had predicted:

"Parliament was rocked again today by scandals involving both the government and the opposition, when four Tory back-bench MPs, two Labour MPs and a senior Cabinet Minister were suspended following new allegations about fraudulent expense claims, which have just come to light. There was a public outcry on social media as it was assumed that this abuse of power had been nipped in the bud in 2009..."

"Another anti-austerity march turned violent today when protesters threw rocks and other missiles at the peace-keeping police presence, and firecrackers at horses carrying mounted officers."

Serghei was asked for comment: "Whilst we cannot condone this sort of violence I am afraid it is an almost inevitable consequence of the policies of a government who have lost touch with real people and their very real problems."

"In a special ITN report tonight we talk to bereaved families who claim that their loved ones have been let down by a failing, under-funded NHS, and are demanding answers from an already beleaguered government."

A concerned looking woman was interviewed. The caption below her said she was Kathryn Jarvis from the Patients' Association: "The major problem seems to be that the custodians of the NHS, our current Tory government, have little interest in providing a free national health service and don't particularly care if it does collapse."

* * *

Sir George had installed a small television set in his personal massage room and sauna. The massage table had a padded window cut out so that anyone lying face down could comfortably rest their face and look down through the window. The TV set was underneath, so that he could get a massage and keep a close eye on the dedicated news channels at the same time. What could be better? He knew of course that it was working-class Tory voters who were their major target, so the news was of great interest as each stage-managed development was reported.

The Spirit of the Nation Party headquarters was buzzing with activity. Keith Taplow had both literally and metaphorically rolled up his sleeves and was right in the thick of it all. Young interns were running round everywhere; expert hackers were slaving over computer keyboards; rows of printers were churning out flyers and posters; film-makers were being briefed on propaganda videos required for social media; a whole noisy room had been set up as a call centre, with rows of young people wearing headsets, handling countless new membership enquiries. Elsewhere Johnnie Collins was animatedly directing his thugs as they piled out of minibuses and vans, creating yet more sensational headline stories for the hungry newsgathering teams:

"There were further outbreaks of civil unrest today, as far apart as Liverpool and Croydon. Austerity protesters set fire to cars, looted stores and were involved in violent clashes with police who resorted to riot sticks, tear gas and water cannons. The government is debating whether to bring in the army to quell any further incidents…"

"There was another embarrassing blow for the government today when a rebellious faction of ten of their own back-bench MPs abstained from a Commons vote, allowing the opposition, with support from the Spirit of the Nation, to defeat their own Prime Minister's bill on privatisation of certain aspects of the NHS and health care…"

"Unless the government steps in and bails them out, a major steelworks in the Rotherham area will have to close next month, it was revealed today. The closure would devastate the community of Templeborough as the factory provides work for almost half the male population of the suburb. A spokesman for the Steelworkers' Union said that his members would take full scale national action if the government did not step up to the plate."

With the government floundering more and more every day, and their Prime Minister looking more and more like a lame duck, a summit meeting was held at the SON headquarters. Sir George Henderson, Keith Taplow, Maz Masters and Serghei Iliescu held crucial talks behind closed doors, sparking the next big news story:

"In a shock statement today the Labour Party and the Spirit of the Nation Party announced they have joined forces to table a vote of no confidence in the government. If the vote goes through it will trigger a snap general election. The last time this happened was in 1979, when James Callaghan was forced to resign as Prime Minister…"

* * *

A week later the doyens of television news were still taking great delight in the intrigue. It seemed that they had become so disillusioned, not to mention bored, by talking about the old two-party system that they were enjoying any departure from the norm as a refreshing change, without delving too deeply into the potential ramifications.

Once again ITN's anchor-man Tom Preston had their political editor June Ellis across his desk. Figuratively speaking, of course.

Preston had a mischievous look on his face. "The dynamic seems to have shifted more than somewhat since the announcement of a snap election last week. Up until now all the long-serving politicians and Westminster die-hards have just sat back and ignored Mr Iliescu, or watched his meteoric rise to power with benign amusement, but all that seems to be changing."

June agreed, "Yes that's certainly true. There has been an almost patronising attitude towards him, like a parent watching their five-year-old-play 'Mummies and Daddies', but suddenly there is real fear that this isn't just a game. My sources from both sides of the House, who insist on remaining anonymous of course, have told me they are worried. One senior Tory figure said she believes Mr Iliescu is 'a serious problem', and a cabinet minister told me he thinks the election will be 'messy'."

Tom raised an eyebrow. "Messy? What did he mean by messy?"

"Messy to them means anything that isn't a fairly clear win by either Labour or the Conservative Party. They actually quite like trading places every few years to be either Punch or Judy. Don't forget they've had things all their own way for nearly a hundred years. The last thing they want is some young upstart spoiling things and robbing them of what they see as their birthright to be either in power or in opposition."

Tom sat back melodramatically. "Gosh, you really think the Spirit of the Nation is that big a threat?"

"Look at the polls. The potential breakdown of the cosy old two-party system is definitely causing a good few sleepless nights in parliamentary circles at the moment."

"So, what's your prediction, June?"

June Ellis grinned knowingly. "Well, we all know, from bitter experience, how wrong the polls can be, but the way things are looking right now I'd say there is a good chance the SON may at least hold the balance of power, which would be a seismic shift in British politics, especially if they get enough seats to have some real clout."

"And will they?"

"The electorate are notoriously fickle when it actually comes to putting that cross in a box, but they just might."

Tom Preston shook his head, smiling with apparent bewilderment, and looked back at his main camera. "Fascinating stuff. June Ellis, thank you very much indeed."

* * *

A few days later Lindsey was back in Wonderland, though sadly there was still no sign of Clive. Instead she was sitting at her favourite table with her ex-boss, newspaper editor Derek Hyland. They had large glasses of wine in front of them, but the mood was far from convivial. Derek looked awkward, and Lindsey looked annoyed at simply being there. Her body language couldn't have been frostier.

"So, how have you been?" enquired Hyland lamely.

Lindsey sighed, "You're not interested in the answer any more than I'm interested in the question. Get to the point. What do you want?"

"I see you haven't lost your social skills. Okay, listen up Lindsey, because I will say this once, and once only. It grieves me to say this, and if you repeat it I will totally deny I ever said it, but... You were right and I was wrong."

Lindsey looked amazed. "About Iliescu?"

"Yes. Beneath the froth and the hype there does seem to be a much darker plan emerging. You're allowed one 'I told you so'."

Lindsey snorted, "Horses and stable doors spring to mind. So are you going to annihilate him at long last?"

"I can't. Sir George insists we remain 'pro', and I've got a terrifying mortgage, exorbitant university fees for my offspring, and a final salary pension plan to consider. But I have a close chum who is editor of a rival broadsheet who have their sights set on taking him down."

Lindsey suddenly looked interested. "Which paper?"

"*The Courier*. I mentioned your name. I'm pretty sure there's a job for you there, if you want it."

The appropriate introductions were made by phone and email, and Lindsey agreed to meet Hyland's more amenable counterpart. They met the following evening in a well-known London pub, which had been the notorious haunt of hard-drinking reporters and journalists since the heyday of Fleet Street. Guy Hartley-Stewart, the rival editor in question, had bought a bottle of red wine, which was on the table between them. The slim, craggy-faced man, of indeterminate middle age, knocked back his glass of wine in one, and immediately replenished it from the bottle.

Lindsey looked startled. "Looks like you needed that."

Guy screwed up his face. "I used to say it's been one of those days, but people pointed out I never seemed to have a good day."

There was a pregnant pause while he took another mouthful of wine.

"You a regular here?" Lindsey asked, somewhat needlessly.

The first wine of the evening seemed to be having the desired effect and Hartley-Stewart visibly relaxed. "Derek speaks very highly of you."

Lindsey harrumphed, "He has a funny way of showing it."

"Selling papers and winning popularity contests rarely go hand in hand. He sells papers."

"You don't have to pander to the lowest common denominator to sell papers."

"No, but it helps. Derek said you were..." Guy paused briefly, choosing his words carefully, "... feisty. That's good, but choose your battles wisely. He's not the enemy here. We are going to need all our energies focussed on the real enemy."

Lindsey looked at him hopefully. "We?"

"There is something much darker going on here than some tabloid celebrity seven-day-wonder."

Lindsey snorted, "I've been saying that for months!"

"And you have also discovered you can't fight this alone. These are dangerous people. Derek's hands are tied. You must see that."

Lindsey looked self-righteous. "*The Courier* seems to have sat on the fence up to now."

Guy looked serious, "We didn't want to join the media circus with all the ballyhoo and celebrity hype, but suddenly this isn't a joke any more. The people pulling the strings are suddenly a real and present threat and they know it, so they are throwing everything they've got at this."

"So what can you throw back?"

"Give me anything you've got to discredit Iliescu. Starting tomorrow we are going to blitz the front page every day until the election."

The battle of the morning headlines became like a tennis match. The *Daily Express* went with 'Is It Time for a Change?', so *The Courier* countered with 'The Evil Spirit of the Nation'. The *Daily Mail* asked 'Is Serghei Inching into the Lead?', *The Courier* answered by saying 'Don't Be Fooled – Iliescu Is a Sham!' *The Sun* led with 'Serghei for Prime Minister!', and *The Courier* called him 'The Biggest Threat to Democracy Since Hitler'.

The Courier got away with this for a few days, but eventually, and inevitably, there came the knock on the door.

It was Guy's wife, Irena Hartley-Stewart, who opened the door to two plain-clothes police officers, accompanied by two uniformed officers. It wasn't the kind of neighbourhood where police cars with flashing lights usually pulled up outside, so Irena was aghast. The detectives showed their warrant cards and entered the elegant Georgian town house, not waiting for an invitation.

Guy was summoned from his summer house at the bottom of the garden. It was one of those heart-stopping moments where one almost goes into shock. Heart racing, cold sweat, awful hollow feeling in the pit of the stomach, words that won't quite articulate. He had no idea what this was about, but it didn't look good. Guy stood there, bewildered, as he faced this intimidating squad. His usual unruffled demeanour deserted him completely as the more senior looking of the two plain-clothes officers consulted her notepad and asked:

"Do you know Christina Townley, Gloria Fellowes and Kate Whitaker?"

His wife suddenly looked even more horrified, clasping her hand over her mouth, second-guessing where this was all leading.

Guy was flustered. "I … they sound… Well, Kate I obviously remember – she was a dancer… We…" He turned to his wife, "Long before I met you."

The detective persisted unrelentingly, "What about the other two? Christina and Gloria?"

"Well, yes, I think… It's a long time ago… I think Tina worked where I was a junior reporter. You're going back a bit."

The detective looked grave. "All three of these women have made serious allegations against you. Accusations of historic sexual offences dating back to the 1980s."

The penny dropped. Guy suddenly looked exasperated. "Right, of course they have. This is all a bit convenient." He turned to his wife again. "I'm being stitched up here, darling, you have to believe me. This is all complete and utter…"

The detective interrupted, "Convenient for who exactly? I'm afraid I'm going to have to ask you to come with us, sir."

"Oh, fuck right off!"

Lindsey watched the evening news in horror as they showed video footage of Guy being led away by the police. It was the lead story. News teams had obviously been tipped off by the police. How else had they known to be there?

The board of directors of *The Courier* had made a statement to say that their editor, Guy Hartley-Stewart, had been suspended with immediate effect, pending Metropolitan Police investigations into serious historic sexual allegations.

Lindsey was still reeling from the shock when the news presenter moved on to the second story of the bulletin:

"In yet another astonishing day in Westminster, three more candidates from traditionally safe Conservative seats have crossed the floor of the House to join the Spirit of the Nation…"

Lindsey felt physically sick.

CHAPTER TWENTY-SEVEN

Maz was beginning to think he liked this lifestyle. Sir George had invited him down to spend another day on the boat. Once again the weather was perfect. Maz was wondering if, in this millionaire's playground in Dorset, they had somehow installed their own climate control system. Perhaps mega-rich people have never actually seen drizzle.

As before, they were sitting on the upper deck, with flocks of seagulls soaring gracefully overhead on the thermals. Maz and Sir George were gazing out over the calm turquoise waters of Poole Bay, occasionally disturbed by the odd foaming bow wave from a ferry taking its cargo of plebeian passengers to Cherbourg or Jersey. Presumably this fabulous motorised yacht could easily overtake them, but then did it ever go anywhere? Or was it just a floating mansion? A ridiculous unnecessary expense.

Of course there was Champagne on ice and orders were being taken for lunch. It would have been rude not to ask for the lobster when they said the chef had been to the fish market that very morning for some fine local specimens.

"I could get used to this," sighed Maz more to himself than to Sir George, picking up his tropical cocktail.

Sir George raised his cocktail glass. "Cheers, dear boy. It's all going really rather well."

Maz wasn't sure whether Sir George was referring to his life in general, or the run-up to the election. Was he wanting to talk 'shop'?

"Your boy is working wonders," Sir George remarked, clarifying matters.

Maz stroked his chin, wondering if this wasn't going to be a free lunch after all. "The whole 'media darling' thing seems to be wearing a bit thin."

Sir George smiled knowingly, "Ah, the media. Have no fears, your boy is bullet-proof."

Maz glanced up. "Apart from his knees, apparently."

"Sorry! Poor analogy. But the people still love him. Fortunately, they don't want to hear a bad word."

Maz looked unsure. "But surely they aren't going to turn that into black-crayoned crosses on ballot slips. Labour and the Tories aren't going to let Golden Bollocks get away with that."

"Naturally both parties are rounding up the party faithful, but that makes the divide between them even greater, so they are splitting the vote against Serghei right down the middle. We only have to get just over a third of the electorate onside and it will be a landslide. A lot less than we had to get behind us to push Brexit through, and see what we did there by appealing to the baser instincts of the great unwashed. In any case, the party faithful aren't quite so faithful when they hear the comprehensive incentive packages and extremely attractive perks of the job offered by the Spirit of the Nation. You've seen the disloyal buggers crossing the floor like greedy ants heading for a honeypot."

Maz sipped his cocktail. "I still think the media are going to turn. It's what they do – build 'em up, then knock 'em back down."

Sir George smiled sardonically. "You do know how much of the media belongs to me?"

"*The Courier* gave him a good hiding last week. Presumably that's not one of yours."

"Ah, *The Courier*. The treacherous Hartley-Stewart. Contrary to popular myth, Mr Masters, even cockroaches can't actually survive the blast from a nuclear warhead."

Maz took a sip of his cocktail. "But surely, at the end of the day, the old guard always wins. The whole British constitution is rigged to protect the system as they've always carved it out. Left and right taking turns, with a few do-gooders and loonies sticking their noses in occasionally, to keep things a bit lively.

But they never win."

Sir George gazed out to sea. "Shall I tell you something interesting about the British Constitution, Mr Masters?"

"Interesting might be stretching things, but go on then, try me."

"There isn't one." Sir George waited for a startled reaction, which was not particularly forthcoming. He ploughed ahead anyway, "We are one of the few countries in the world who don't have a written constitution. Even the need for a British Prime Minister is not written in stone. It's a historic tradition, if you like, more than a constitutional requirement. If we can get enough MPs in the house to fast-track a couple of new Acts of Parliament we can turn the whole shooting-match on its head... and make your boy unshiftable from the top job! Just like Trump wished for, but couldn't achieve, because, unlike Britain, they do have a rock-solid constitution."

Maz did react this time. "Fuck me! No wonder they called that telly programme *House of Cards*."

* * *

As the snap general election approached, the TV news teams were going into overdrive. Once again they were wallowing far more in the gossip from the corridors of power and all the gamesmanship, without bothering to analyse the potential consequences. Tom Preston and political editor June Ellis from ITN had daily discourses on the subject:

"So where are we with the polls at the moment, June?"

"Well it's very close, but the suggestion is that Serghei and the Spirit of the Nation aren't quite there yet. If the polls are to be believed then they wouldn't quite have a majority."

"Isn't that pretty much exactly what the polls said about Brexit and Donald Trump, first time around?"

June laughed, "Well yes, but this is a remarkable state of affairs. The SON will almost certainly hold the balance of power after the election, which, in itself, is ground-breaking."

* * *

In Serghei's apartment there were newspapers strewn everywhere. Maz had brought round that day's tabloid and broadsheet offerings, like he did every day. Just about every single paper carried photos and headlines on their front pages regarding Serghei's election prospects, hopes and dreams. Serghei was spreading the newspapers out and thumbing through them all.

"All this is good for feeding my ego."

Maz, who was gazing out of the window, deep in thought, replied, "Butcher's dog springs to mind."

Serghei frowned, still dissatisfied. "But I think George and Keith only ever let me say what they want me to say."

Maz turned to face his protégé. "Ultimately, my friend, you have the power. You can say anything you like when you're the one with the microphone. Toe the line for now. We let them make you irreplaceable and then we'll worry about changing the agenda."

Later that day Maz was making his way back to his Wardour Street office from a cab which had dropped him off on the corner of the block. Nobody passing would have even noticed, it was done so expertly by the two heavy-set, yet unobtrusive men, but he was bundled against his will into the back of a large, black, four-by-four vehicle with dark one-way windows. The SUV sped off as soon as he and his assailants were on board. The whole kidnapping took less than forty seconds, right outside his own office complex, with a minimum of fuss. The secret had been the element of surprise.

An hour later Maz was on the dirty floor of a disused south London warehouse, curled up in the foetal position, taking a vicious kicking.

"Not the head or the face," Keith Taplow said, watching impassively. "For now."

Maz groaned and writhed as the painful kicks to his abdomen, back and chest abated for a moment.

Taplow was keeping a safe distance from the unsavoury business, looking down at his smartphone screen, and selecting an app. "Now, you are probably wondering what this is all about. The thing is you really mustn't go putting silly ideas into your boy's head, Mr Masters."

Maz coughed and spat a little blood before hoarsely saying, "I have no idea what you're going on about."

"No Cockney barrow-boy banter? How refreshing. To save a lot of pointless and time-wasting denials allow me to play you this recording from earlier today."

Taplow pressed the button on the screen of his phone and Maz heard his own voice, *We let them make you irreplaceable and then we'll worry about changing the agenda..."* The recording was stopped.

"Fuck me!" gasped Maz. "You've got his place bugged."

"Have you any idea how much we have invested in Serghei?" Taplow snarled. "Of course we've got his place bugged! He can't break wind without us knowing."

"Jesus!" groaned Maz, curling up again on the floor, giving in to the pain.

"I suggest you tread very carefully from now on, Masters. Sir George and I have vastly differing views regarding your indispensability."

Maz still had some defiance not quite beaten out of him. "Serghei still listens to me. He doesn't trust you bastards."

"Then I suggest you persuade him to trust us. You see we have been keeping a close eye on you as well – Stanley. Perhaps we should tell Serghei what really happened to his first wife, Aurelia. He thinks she's back in Romania, doesn't he? And then there's Simona's tragic story. You have been a busy boy, covering his tracks. Busy boy, but naughty boy."

Maz looked defeated as he lay there on the floor, designer suit covered in blood and dust, clutching his bruised, possibly cracked ribs.

Fortunately for Maz, Taplow's phone rang.

"Get him up and get him out of here," Taplow ordered, snapping his fingers at the two thugs and waving towards the door. He'd seen that the caller was Sir George, so he had to take the call. Moving swiftly away from the scene of Maz's grisly warning he swiped the screen of his phone.

"George. How are you? Me? Oh, just taking care of a little pest control. Nothing for you to worry about."

CHAPTER TWENTY-EIGHT

In the run-up to the imminent general election, June Ellis, ITN's political editor, was conducting a series of in-depth interviews with the main party leaders. The basic studio set had *Leaders Election Special* emblazoned across the back. There had been a heated debate with the set designer whether 'leaders' should have an apostrophe, and, if so, where it should go. In the end they agreed, stylistically, not to bother. Serghei was in his wheelchair, facing his turn for a TV grilling.

June leaned forward intently, making direct eye contact with Serghei. "The Spirit of the Nation Party manifesto talks about 'a robust new immigration policy' and 'special deportation powers'. This is potentially inflammatory stuff, Mr Iliescu."

Serghei looked calm and collected. He had been well-briefed and extensively rehearsed. "Inflammatory for people who are here for the wrong reasons, yes. Listen – we intend to tackle the terrorist problem once and for all. No more pussy-footing. God-fearing, ordinary, decent people, who live in this country for the right reasons, will thank us for it."

Ms Ellis tackled another controversial issue. "You also talk about creating a task force to help implement a zero-tolerance policy."

"Yes, with greater powers than the police, to deal with vicious gang crime, which is totally out of control in our major cities. They will also tackle all forms of terrorism and the war on drugs and people-trafficking."

June looked concerned. "Greater powers than the police? Will they be armed?"

Serghei looked non-committal. "More so than the police are."

"Are we talking about martial law here?"

"Of course not. But we have to make British streets safe to walk. Our children deserve peace of mind and protection, don't they? Anybody with nothing to hide will have nothing to fear. The Great British public want somebody to make those tough decisions and take a stance. It is time for change and time for decent people to take back control."

* * *

The next day Keith Taplow received yet another phone call from high command.

Sir George Henderson didn't waste time with small-talk. "According to the latest informed predictions it's still not in the bag yet. Time is running out. You know a part of me has been praying that this moment would never become necessary, but is it contemptible of me to confess the adrenalin rush right now is making me feel more alive than I've ever been? It's time to shock the complacent fuckers into the polling stations."

Taplow took a breath. This was momentous, even for him, "We're all standing-by and prepared."

"Then I'm unleashing the Apocalypse."

Four days later there was breaking news. It appeared on the internet first, then TV news bulletins gave grave announcements:

"Emergency services are attending two major incidents. Reports are coming in of large explosions in central areas of Manchester and London. They appear to be the results of bombs being detonated and, although no group has yet claimed responsibility, both incidents have similarities and bear the hallmarks of terrorist attacks. Just days before the general election it would appear that these coordinated attacks have been orchestrated to disrupt the democratic process. Exact numbers are not yet known, but there are multiple casualties and some fatalities in both locations. We go live now – first to Manchester…"

* * *

From that sickening day until the general election, social media was flooded with propaganda videos showing distressing images of the bomb attacks in Manchester and London, intercut with shots of Serghei saying: "We intend to tackle the terrorist problem once and for all"; "We have to make British streets safe to walk"; "Our children deserve peace of mind and protection"; "God-fearing, ordinary, decent people, who live in this country for the right reasons, will thank us for it"; "The Great British public want somebody to make those tough decisions and take a stance"; "It is time for change and time for decent people to take back control…"

This was digital-age brainwashing on an industrial scale. It was unwittingly helped by the major television channels repeating everything they could lay their hands on featuring Serghei the miracle worker, and of course every newspaper, whether it was owned by Sir George or not, splashed Serghei all over the front pages. Free will didn't stand a chance.

* * *

The morning after election day everybody, but everybody, was watching the morning news, featuring the all-important results:

"In the past twenty-four hours history has been made. Although there are a handful of constituencies still to declare, it is now clear that the British people have decided, and have voted for a new kind of politics. The Spirit of the Nation will have a large majority in the House of Commons, and Serghei Iliescu will be the next British Prime Minister. It has been a disastrous night for both Labour and Conservatives. The old two-party system is dead. The electorate have voted for change. It just remains to be seen how radical that change will be. Serghei Iliescu has a large enough majority to dictate terms for a new Britain."

Around half the country watched in disbelief, some in horror, including Lindsey, Derek and Guy. The other half were jubilant and in celebratory mood, feeling energised and liberated. Maz watched in dismay, resigned to the inevitable, as he watched the Prime Minister make a tearful farewell speech outside Downing Street, her husband at her side. Sir George Henderson was face down on his massage table watching the small television set on the floor, through the padded window in the table, with immense satisfaction. Slowly, he turned to lie on his back and gave his personal masseuse a knowing nod.

Sir George just loved a happy ending.